Among the Bones

A Novel

Donna Koros Stramella

Quill Hawk Publishing

ISBN: 979-8-9879719-2-5 paperback
Jacket designed by Virginia McKevitt & Jenny Muscatell
Printed in the United States of America
Library of Congress Control Number: 2023920740

Contents

To Sarah and Christa with my love

Prologue

Six-feet under was always deeper than he remembered. Smoke from another distant wildfire drifted across the late evening sky, lace filtering an ivory half-moon. In the dim light he paused, leaning against the shelf of dirt as he considered, "How long would it take to dig the last foot? Or was this deep enough?"

His eyes adjusted further to the darkness, and his body reclaimed its energy. He didn't get this far without careful planning. "Six-feet," he recited to himself like a mantra. "Follow the plan."

After the first, he'd learned the hard way that such a depth in one night was too much. Too much for one man trying to complete a singular mission in a single night. Since then, there was always a prep grave on standby, covered with a tangle of brush. No one roamed through this forgotten area. It was his personal secret garden with flowers hidden beneath the surface.

"Follow the plan," he recited again, thinking of the new flower in his garden. This one was less flashy than the others. Still, there was a certain something about her--maybe her chiseled cheekbones--that made her exceptional. Now she would remain exceptional. The longer she lived, the greater the chance she'd become ordinary, even ruined. Her color faded, her dried petals chipped and brown.

He was always careful with his delicate flowers. No visible cuts or bruises. Their hair would mask any swelling or discoloration, although sometimes he miscalculated his strength. A few bled, and he carefully wiped the blood from their hair before cradling them in new blankets.

Thinking about this one and the others before renewed his strength, and he dug faster, deeper. He liked to think about his girls, safe and peaceful.

There would be no graveside mourners, no markers etched with "devoted daughter," no flowers placed here on birthdays. Still, they had each other. A sorority of sorts. And the initiation didn't drag on for weeks, forcing them to give away a little of themselves with each requirement.

The girls in this garden were specially selected, and the initiation was quick. He spoke to them first so they'd understand his mission. And then just a single calculated blow to the back of the head.

Chapter 1

The whole town knew Ruth was a good girl. Faithfully attended Mass every Sunday and visited her family after. Displayed perfect customer service at work. Dressed without flourish, favoring medium neutral tones. Even her face did not counter this mild reputation—symmetrical but nondescript, olive eyes with a light swipe of mascara on her lashes, wavy chestnut brown hair kept shoulder length, and bangs slightly long to cover a clover-shaped birth mark low on her forehead. From Ruth's view, her only defining feature was a prominent natural blonde streak that fell on the right side of her face.

She rarely wore jewelry except for a rotation of three pairs of earrings—tiny gold hoops, mother-of-pearl posts, and short crystal dangles. She almost always wore her large cross necklace, but kept it tucked inside her clothes because of its size.

How would Ruth describe her best self? Independent. Confident. Brave. She repeated those words in her mind, as she woke and as she drifted off to sleep. As though repetition would force those traits to materialize.

Those who knew her would describe her as quiet, gentle, and good. Someone who should be pitied. Ruth was the only person still alive who knew those assessments were wrong.

Mass was over at St. Lawrence Martyr and she kissed her Great Aunt Indy goodbye before making her way to the front. As was her custom she put a few dollars in the metal slot, then lit five candles, keeping her eyes on the ribbons of red and orange light. Her stomach rose to her chest. Her heart beat faster. The stiff carpet scratched her bare knees as she folded her hands across her waist and said five prayers. Finally looking away from the flames, she rose and moved to the entrance area, blessing herself with the holy water from the brass font by the door, and then shaking Father Anthony's hand.

"It's a glorious day, isn't it Ruth?"

"Truly, Father. Enjoy your Sunday!"

It had been some time since she'd visited Father Anthony, or even felt the need. Ruth counted that as a win. Or maybe she'd just given up.

She skirted by two elderly couples, the Smyths and the Pattersons who all swiveled their heads in her direction. She could hear their unspoken "Poor Ruth" as she nodded and smiled before descending the marble steps and turning right on the tree-lined sidewalk toward her first stop—Blooms Flower Stand on Madison and Anchor streets. Ruth pulled out folded bills from her blue wristlet to purchase five flowers. Usually roses, but sometimes dahlias for a change.

"Which will it be, Ruth? Both the roses and dahlias look splendid right now." The owner, Mrs. Bloomsberry (a fortunate name for a florist) reduced the price for all regular customers, but Ruth thought the discount was yet another display of pity. Just like the owner of the pharmacy who gave her a job after junior college graduation. Just like the next-door neighbor who invited her to tea in her garden once a month in the spring and summer. Just like her Aunt Indy who took her in and protected her. Among Ruth's long list of fears, being pitied was near the top.

Ruth looked carefully at the flowers, judging their freshness. "I think the roses again, Mrs. Bloomsberry. The apricot shade looks especially bright this week."

The walk was cheerful today, with a bright sun and willowy breeze that carried sweet scents. Early spring flowers were in bloom, daffodils and tulips in gardens with tall groupings of fireweed in the back, and blossoming cherry and pear trees shading the sidewalk. She almost enjoyed her weekly walks during this time of year. Next would come summer, with new flowers crowding gardens, then autumn with the orange, yellow, and slightly burned leaves that crunched under her worn brown leather shoes.

Winter was not so pleasant. The winds off the harbor blew the snow into drifts. The temperatures dipped below freezing. The flower stand closed for the season. Still, Ruth made her weekly visits, regardless of the weather.

She could likely follow the route in darkness by memory and intuition. The periodic drops in the sidewalk, the scent of the pines. The route was baked into every cell of her body, so she found her way, even in the thick fog and heavy snow. Really, it was the least she could do, and she sometimes convinced herself, at least for that moment, that her rituals would bring redemption.

There was a short break in the trees, and Ruth looked up, squinting. Today's sky was lighter than yesterday's. Maybe more bleached by the sun. Her chunky block heals clicked along on the cement, and she felt the pressure. The padding had thinned. She sighed. Among her mental list of hated chores—shoe shopping. It didn't help that there was only one shoe shop in town, owned by the kind, but incredibly slow Mr. Blakeshire. Despite the thick glasses that he'd worn for the last decade, his low vision slowed him even further.

On her last visit, he'd brought out the first box of wrong-sized shoes, followed by the second, followed by the third in the right size, but wrong style. Maybe she'd try ordering online this time. Although she was sure Mr. Blakeshire could use the business. And she didn't want to disappoint him, or anyone for that matter. As if treating everyone with kindness would help if her secret was discovered.

After she passed the particularly unruly cluster of trees, she saw the entrance in view. So grand.

A couple of years ago, the caretaker had a stroke, and the heavy iron gates had been locked when she arrived. On that day, she'd circled around, finding a spot where the fence was loose and pulling it back to enter, walking by a neglected area with small headstones labeled "Trixie" and "Pepper." The long-abandoned pet cemetery. The area was overgrown and hidden behind a cluster of pines. Her foot had sunk into the mud by the final resting place of "Lucy" and she'd envisioned a small spaniel with wiry auburn hair. As she'd transitioned to the single-lane road, Ruth scraped the thick mud off her shoes, walking by all of the other sites and back to the small wrought iron marker with Jesus and the sheep that marked the turn to Good Shepherd Drive.

Today, the gates were open as usual, shadows from the ornate inset casting a swirling pattern on the ground. She'd been doing this for ten years--a full 520 weeks--all the way back to the time when everything had changed.

In the early years, she was happy to have company. After Mass, her mother's Aunt Indy held her hand when they walked over to the memorial candles, helping her steady the long taper to light all five candles. She helped her select the freshest blooms from the flower stand and stood behind her as Ruth knelt on the soft grass for a respectful amount of time, remembering their goodness, one by one, and always in order of their ages.

Bo Samuel Sagmire

October 12, 1970 – December 27, 2008

When she closed her eyes, she could see her father's ruddy complexion and blonde waves that fell over his forehead and sometimes into his eyes if he waited too long to ask Ruth's mother to cut his hair. His broad shoulders and tall build. His hands with rough patches like the pre-sanded wood he crafted into custom cabinets. She could almost smell the maple and taste the wood dust that floated inside his workshop.

Maryanne Olivia Sagmire
June 15, 1972 - December 27, 2008

Ruth smelled lavender when she pictured her mother. Practical and frugal by necessity, her mother's one indulgence was to place a dot of lavender cologne from the pharmacy behind each ear in the morning. She was petite with straight brown hair that fell on her shoulders, and bangs pushed slightly to the side. In Ruth's mind, her mother wore the plain purple apron Ruth made in Home Economics class, a gift for Christmas that year. Her mother was baking honey-almond cookies, a lattice apple pie, a black-walnut cake. Or one of her many specialties that filled the house with sweet scents on especially cold days. Days when they all crowded near the warm oven in anticipation of goodness.

Lilly Anne Sagmire
December 3, 1999 - December 27, 2008

Three years younger than Ruth and 12 minutes older than her identical twin, Catherine. Most people couldn't tell her sisters apart, but Ruth could. Lilly cocked her head slightly to the left when she listened. On her fourth birthday, she'd fallen on the rock driveway, resulting in a small gash on her upper right cheek—another distinguishing feature. And there was a reflection in the twins' eyes that differed, although Ruth couldn't say exactly what it was. They had the same wavy blonde hair as their father, the same polite laugh as their mother. Lilly always seemed to be missing, as she sought out the quietest spot on the property, a library book in her hand.

Catherine Olivia Sagmire

December 3, 1999 - December 27, 2008

Catherine was regarded as the animal expert in her family. She was up early to collect the eggs each morning, singing to the chickens and giving each a gentle pat on their head. The stray cats who collected field mice around the house responded only to Catherine and would approach her as she set fresh water at the bottom of the porch steps. Twice, when neighborhood dogs wandered off, it was Catherine who managed to find them. She was excited easily, and clapped her hands gently to express happiness.

Samuel Matthew Sagmire

October 5, 2002 - December 27, 2008

The twins had each other, but Ruth had Sam. As each year passed, she cried a little less as she thought about her family. But memories of Sam were still the most painful. Six was his permanent age. He had brown hair like her and eyes perpetually opened wide. His whole being lit up when he did something he loved, especially eating their mother's fruit pies. Ruth smiled briefly, thinking of him lifting his fork in the air before he ate the first bite. He made up funny rhymes and drew stick figure cartoons on napkins and scraps of paper. Sometimes she allowed herself to consider who Sam might have become. An artist. A loving father. Maybe someone who was famous for his baked pies.

Each week, it was harder to visualize the details. Took her longer to accurately recall Sam's crooked front tooth (was it the right or the left?), the two different reflections in her sisters' eyes.

Among the uniform markers, one did not include a name or dates. The blank marker was nestled between her mother and Catherine. A space that should have been filled 10 years ago. This one was saved for Ruth.

Sometimes she stared at her space and thought of the hardness of the earth. Other times she thought about the coolness of the grass and imagined being cushioned beneath. She thought about rejoining her family. She thought about the end date—the only one that would be different from the rest. And Ruth always thought that no one would ever visit her family again. No one would ever buy the prettiest flower to place on her grave.

She had been alone on her visits for some time, ever since Aunt Indy's leg cramps took hold and prevented her from walking any serious distance. They lived just around the corner from the church, so her aunt and grown cousins and their families all met there on Sunday morning. A substitute family. Ruth's time with her own family was now a solitary time, although she once heard her aunt try to persuade her eldest daughter Martha to go with Ruth.

"It's creepy," Martha said in a whispered tone that was still loud enough to hear from the top of the staircase. "I mean, I get why she goes. But every week? It's just not normal."

Another fear to add to Ruth's list. People would think she was odd. Or maybe they already did. Although recently she thought that might not be true. Certainly, the rich developer Bill Rafferty didn't think her abnormal, although his generosity was certainly laced with pity. Still, she could hear her father's gravelly voice in her head saying, "Don't look a gift horse in the mouth, even though there might be a hidden cost."

It was a rather unusual offer. One she couldn't ignore. She still rented a room from her aunt, and her job as a pharmacy tech at the small drug store would never provide the kind of income she'd need to buy something in Heritage Hill. And moving elsewhere wasn't an option. She could never leave.

Ruth was twenty-two. Who would turn down a free house in a town where everyone wanted to live? Where most people couldn't afford to live? A free house in a brand-new community where she already spent a lot of time. A familiar place with familiar people. With the people she missed the most.

She instantly knew she would accept the offer, if only to avoid disappointing Mr. Rafferty.

Even so, his promise that her house would be in view of the family plot had caused a chill to settle in her back. The thought both comforted and terrified her. Before, she only atoned once a week for the gravest of sins. Now she'd have to seek forgiveness every day.

Chapter 2

Bill Rafferty looked closely at his photo in the Business Section of *USA Today*. He knew his gelled-back dark brown hair and sharp features stereotyped him as an undertaker, and he was glad to project added credibility. His forty-five years looked more like fifty in the picture, but he decided a seasoned, wiser appearance was beneficial for his brand.

He was CEO of Rafferty Enterprises, an uninspired name for (as he often said) an inspired company. And now there was national news coverage as proof. Not just local or state interest, but the whole U.S. of A. He pictured thousands of hotel guests around the country, picking up their complimentary *USA Today* newspaper when they opened their doors to the hallway, tucking it under their arms as they followed the sweet scent of freshly pressed waffles to the breakfast buffet downstairs. While they ate their ordinary powdered eggs and drank their ordinary domestic coffee, they would encounter the extraordinary when they opened their newspapers.

Ruth was the linchpin for this outstanding coverage. Young, casually pretty, humble, and with a heartbreaking history. She was reluctant about the publicity, but Bill Rafferty knew his generosity would inspire (or guilt) her into the interviews.

When he thought back, it was easy to see how everything fit. Why everything in his life happened. All leading to the inevitable: the most talked about and (if he was honest, which he told everyone he was) the most envied real estate project in recent history. Or maybe ever. Affordable housing. Small carbon footprint. Sense of community. He didn't care about those positive attributes, only that those talking points brought favorable press, city approval, and public interest.

This hard-fought gain started many years ago with a loss. Although some people may see it more as a setback or disadvantage rather than pure loss. It took him some pain and time to figure out the difference between the two, and he eventually decided his forward motion started with a clear-cut loss.

His grappling to understand loss started in first grade, when his classmate James' parents died in a helicopter crash during their 10th anniversary trip to Hawaii. Everyone called it a loss. *Poor James, he's lost everything. He's lost the two most important people in the world. He's lost the only life he knew.* The words made him curious, so when James returned to school after a brief absence, young Bill stared at his friend whenever he could privately do so. He didn't look any different. Same freckled nose, same crooked teeth, same wild red hair. No sign that anything was missing.

Bill returned home after school each day to the small condo he shared with his mother Gretchen, who was younger than the other mothers at school. She was only 17 when he was born.

No one ever mentioned his father. And when Bill was much older, he requested a copy of his birth certificate. The *father* block was empty.

Still, the young boy lived in a nice complex in a quiet neighborhood. No doubt paid for by his mother's brother George, because Gretchen didn't have a job. Bill once heard his mother tell a friend over the phone: "My family knows I'm too fragile to work." And she was. More specifically, her mind was.

There was a slow, downward progression that replayed in Bill's mind even though he tried to shut it down. Her daily showers went to alternate days, to weekly.

Eventually, she hid the soap from Bill, insisting that "the bar is full of chemicals that will poison you." Trips to the grocery store followed the same pattern. Eventually, his mother only purchased canned vegetables and meat, stating that the government regularly sprayed local farmers' fields to make people sick. "That's how they keep the population in check."

Her rantings to her son, people over the phone, and neighbors unlucky enough to see her at the entrance mailbox grew louder and longer. During those months when the showers decreased and the rants increased, Uncle George upped his monthly visits to weekly, and eventually to every day. He brought Bill supplies to keep in a box under his bed—packages of nuts, breakfast bars, cardboard juice packets, soap, shampoo.

Although Bill stayed in his room as requested, the conversations between his mother and her brother were clear. George wanted his sister to visit a doctor and start taking meds. When Gretchen learned her brother was making arrangements for her to spend some time in a *facility*, she disappeared, leaving everything behind—including her son.

Uncle George and Aunt Jo tried to find her. They called her old friends who hadn't spoken to her for months. They knocked on each door in the building. They searched nearby parks and called hospitals. They filed a missing person report. After three months of a full-press search there seemed to be a heavy, collective sigh followed by no further mention of her name. Whether it was a sigh of regret or a sigh of relief, Bill would never know. But what he did finally know was loss.

He had a good life going forward, but he always felt a part of him was missing. There were distant happy memories. His mother taking him to the park, the two of them going down the big slide together, her legs squeezing in on both sides to keep him safe. Trips to the farmer's market where she showed him how to spot perfectly ripe green apples, and how to peel back the husk to find corn with the most uniform rows. Those happy memories were the ones that he stored in the front of his mind. The other memories, after the downward progression started, were pushed to the back, like some dusty box in the dark corner of the attic. He tried not to look there. As each year passed, he found it easier to forget those memories existed.

He moved in with Uncle George and Aunt Jo. His clothes were outgrown by then, so they took him shopping for new ones. They bought him a new bookbag and lunchbox. Everything was now divided by old and new, except for one thing. On the Monday after his mother's disappearance, he was back in his first-grade classroom sitting next to Sam. Now they were both members of the same sad club, the club of people who lived in the new, but still knew there was an old.

The big Victorian house on the corner of Madison and Port bore no similarity to the small apartment building. But he was glad both houses were located in the Heritage school district. And even though he and Sam never talked about the old, there was comfort in knowing someone else understood there were two lives.

In the big house, Bill had a significantly larger bedroom. One that easily held imposing-looking, dark-wood matching furniture--four-poster bed, armoire, large dresser with mirror, and two bedside tables. There was a window cut in under the eaves, with a built-in bench seat covered in a red-striped pattern that Aunt Jo picked out. Bill hated red. But he mostly liked his room and the house, which he also shared with his aunt and uncle's two cats—Paprika and Pepper. He shared the house with others as well. Guests. That's what his aunt and uncle called them.

On the day he moved in, there was an elderly woman with tightly-curled grey hair and a stubborn look on her face. She left after two days. The next arrivals were a teenaged boy with matted blonde hair and a woman in her forties with a shaved head. The guests lived on the first floor of the house. The main living quarters on the second and third floors were strictly off limits to the guests. Still, his aunt and uncle spent many hours on the first floor, interacting not only with the guests, but with their visitors as well. From the floors above, he would often hear quiet conversation, and frequently the sound of crying. Bill thought the sounds as background noise, even though Paprika and Pepper usually ventured out from their hiding places when they heard sobs. They jumped up beside Bill when he was reading or finishing schoolwork. One or the other pushed its way under his book to settle on his lap or leaned its head over on his leg. He knew from experience that if he started to pet them for more than a few seconds, they'd hop off. He'd learned to settle for a quick pat.

As the months went on, Bill was allowed more time on the first floor as well. Often to assist with opening or closing the heavy door. To direct people to the visiting parlor. To take coats and umbrellas. To offer a tissue or a glass of water. In truth, he enjoyed meeting the new guests, hearing their stories and looking at their pictures. And the fact that he lived above a funeral parlor never made him feel anxious. Sometimes he felt more at ease with the guests than he did with himself.

Chapter 3

Ruth felt uncomfortable with the request. She thought about declining, even considered a few excuses. Once again, guilt silenced her. That and her father's voice in her head, stating emphatically, "There's no such thing as a free lunch!" Funny, she'd never understood all those sayings he tried to impress on her when she was younger. They were tucked away in her mind, and at just the right moment the right one would spill out, like exact change clinking in the metal return of a vending machine.

The wealthy families in Coastal View had been generous to the Sagmire family. While the other families grew in wealth with each passing year, the Sagmire's finances moved in the other direction.

Still, people thought highly of the family. The gift of a used vehicle. Swimming lessons for all the children, sailing lessons for Ruth. Clothes, furniture, and even appliances. Her mother was amazed by the fully useable items people replaced, just to have the "latest and greatest." Ruth's father took a more cynical view. Soon after those generous gifts appeared a request followed, like a cabinet that needed an exact replacement. A custom-made door in need of refinishing. A failed DIY project that screamed for a professional carpenter. "Repayment," her father would scoff, usually shaking his head. "Why don't they just tell me upfront instead of trying to look like they're doing us a favor?"

For Ruth, the concept of a free lunch equaled a free house. So Ruth agreed to the request. As her repayment for his generosity, she would speak with the press. She would deliver a homemade cake (a box mix was close enough) to each of her new neighbors with a reporter, photographer, or both alongside her. The press would start immediately, but the cakes would come later. So far, Ruth's house was the only one complete, with others in various stages of construction. She would be the first living resident of Coastal View, which would now house more than just the dead.

Her aunt expressed concern that Ruth would the only resident for at least two weeks and suggested she wait before taking occupancy. But Mr. Rafferty assured his most important homeowner that security was already in place. So there Ruth sat at the settlement table, feeling very small in such a large conference room.

"I guess there's nothing left but to sign," she said, lifting her voice to as brave a tone as possible, hoping to mask the cracking as she spoke. With her aunt hovering at her side, Ruth signed carefully on the line at each red X, realizing that her signature would be captured forever. Susan, the woman from the title company who sat across from her, briefly explained what each signature indicated. Aunt Indy listened intently, then nodded at Ruth as though her great niece needed her wise guidance to proceed. In truth, she understood little since she'd always left such paperwork to her husband, now long deceased.

With the last signature in place, Susan rose, extending her arm to shake Ruth's hand. "Congratulations! The first homeowner at Coastal View. Quite an accomplishment."

"Thank you," Ruth said pleasantly, but all the while thinking about the word *accomplishment*. What did she accomplish to earn a free house? Losing her whole family? Her mind started to wander further into that dark place, and she felt a familiar chill start to form in her back until her aunt spoke.

"All complete? I'm ready for the lunch you promised me, Ruth."

"Of course, Aunt Indy," she smiled. "It's time to celebrate."

Aunt Indy shuffled forward awkwardly, using her newly-acquired cane. They were almost out of the conference room when Susan startled them with the urgency in her voice.

"Wait! I forgot the most important part," she said, walking quickly to Ruth. "Here are your keys."

"Well, yes! I suppose I'll need those," she said. "Although I won't be moving in until after tomorrow's big unveiling."

"Hmph," Aunt Indy said with a clear annoyance in her voice, her forehead creasing. "I suppose people will be traipsing through your new home?"

Ruth blushed and lowered her eyes.

"People will be having a look," Ruth said. "But Mr. Rafferty has a cleaning company lined up for the day after. Full, deep clean the very next morning."

Aunt Indy started moving forward, seemingly satisfied about the arrangement and now thinking about lunch again. When they were alone in the hallway, her aunt turned toward her with an uncharacteristic expression forming on her usually steadfast face. Her lips pressed so hard together they were hidden. The start of tears in her eyes.

"Dear girl, I do want you to know," she said, reaching out to hold her great niece's hand. "I want you to know that it wasn't about obligation. I may not say it often, but I love you."

"I love you too, Aunt Indy."

"Your presence, when my children were all going their own ways…I wasn't just there for you, my dear. You were there for me."

"That's sweet of you to say."

Her aunt took a breath, gripping Ruth's hand a little tighter. "It's more than that. I suppose your arrival gave me a sense of purpose, a reason to be. I hope you'll still need me, or at least pretend to need me sometime."

"I promise," Ruth said, not indicating that she would be pretending.

Aunt Indy seemed to command the forming tears back up into the recesses of her eyes, then gave her head a little shake. "Enough of this self-serving sentimentality then—I simply must eat something or I'll collapse!"

Chapter 4

The crowds surprised and delighted him. Rafferty paid off-duty police officers to manage any unexpected issues, especially from the families of current residents—those permanently interned in Coastal View. Fortunately, such unpleasantness didn't emerge, so the police were pressed into new service handing out quickly-generated time slot tickets to manage the numbers. They added another hour, but still turned potential future residents away who didn't expect a wait.

Looking back, it was his careful planning--national press, partnerships with Silicon Valley employers, and a social media campaign. He'd hired one of the best PR firms in the state, knowing the exorbitant fees would pay off. If not for this flagship project, for two other Pacific northwest communities (part of stage two development) and five additional U.S. deals (stage three)—all negotiated or underway. Stage four planning focused on international markets in crowded, popular cities like Tokyo. And stage five introduced franchises. Long-term interest depended on Coastal

View's success, which meant nothing must be missed—except the overwhelming attendance on preview day. Certainly a positive, but a reminder to always consider the unexpected.

Coastal View had multiple advantages, including the obvious—he was the sole deed holder. It was quiet and safe. There had been only two incidents of minor vandalism, but that was more than a dozen years ago, before the gates were installed at the entrance. From those custom-designed black-iron scrolled gates (now with a scanner for entry), the new residents could take a 5-10 minute stroll into town. Local restaurants, a busy pub, charter fishing, sailing, kayaking, and relaxing in lovely Heritage beach park. The community was in the right zip code, one of the most sought-after in the nation. Houses were handed down from generation to generation, limiting listings and driving up prices. The last house that sold, six months prior, listed for $2.5 million. Interest drove up the final price even higher. It was a neglected three-bedroom, one-bath. No view from the single story, but just a block from the waterfront. More than aesthetic repairs. Old plumbing. Caving roof. Electrical system failing. The new owners tore down the house and paid another million-plus to build a four-story, giving them a wide view of the bay.

For the largest real estate company in town, waiting lists grew upwards of 200. Agents tried steering clients toward nearby communities, but these were people accustomed to the best, so they were willing to wait for the Heritage zip code.

Despite its name, the community of Coastal View didn't have a water view. Maybe if the tall pines that propagated Heritage were razed, there would be a peek of the bay from the entrance. But those pines weren't going anywhere, since the city council kept an almost parental watch over its native trees.

The Heritage City Council. A formidable threshold for Rafferty, and one he had been required to cross. Despite predictions to the contrary, his request passed on the first vote. Most residents were shocked by the ease of such an unusual variance.

What was deemed as "flash success" by the local newspaper was a naïve view. A patient man, his work to gain approval started long before the vote. He cultivated close friendships and symbiotic business arrangements, all aimed at his end goal. It would have been obvious to court current members of the council. Instead, he courted individuals he saw positioned for power in the community, years before they were elected to the council. He didn't need a unanimous decision. The vote was seven for, five against, split between the newest electees and the old guard who never saw it coming.

There was one more significant hurdle. The current residents of Coastal View. Not the current residents themselves, which would be quite impossible. But rather their families. He knew neither money nor friendship would counteract their refusals. Instead, he turned to the tried and true: fear.

Over the last decade, horrific crimes were committed at cemeteries, albeit in other areas of the country. Graves desecrated, gravestones spray painted or broken, bodies dug up and removed. Whether by a single individual at each, or a group of individuals roaming the country, no one knew. Rafferty played up the second. A group, better yet, a cult of twisted devotees stealing bodies from their final resting places.

On a long Sunday drive with a single purpose, he exited the interstate and used a burner phone to call the local newspaper. As he knew, there would be no one to take his call on a Sunday, so he left a brief scripted message on the voice mail. An anonymous tip. The cult ravaging graves in other areas of the country was headed to Heritage.

On Monday, the initial story ran on the inside front cover. *An anonymous tip was received at The Herald indicating that a group desecrating graves in other areas of the country may now be heading to Heritage. The Herald is working closely with local law enforcement, and will provide additional details as available.*

TheHerald, energized by such a tantalizing story ran it on the front page the rest of the week, with more detail about previous incidents and quotes from investigators in those areas. Saturday's above the fold story included a quote by Mr. William "Bill" Rafferty, the owner of Coastal View: "We will take all measures necessary to continue to protect the beloved in our care, and their visiting loved ones." He met with the residents' families, as well as others who owned burial sites. And he proposed two distinct options.

Option one: the addition of a twenty-four-hour guard at the entrance, funded by the owners or their families.

Option two: Rafferty Enterprises would build small residences along the border of the actual burial areas. The addition of a new part-time security position would be funded by these new homeowners. He knew this idea would be novel and creative to some, bizarre and disturbing to others. Still, this option ensured no additional costs to the families or the future residents.

Whether the families preferred the second option because it was free or because it was more in line with the peaceful surroundings, he never knew and didn't care. The decision was close, but the terms in contracts signed by each purchaser were clear—widespread changes would be decided by a majority vote.

A unanimous vote would have made life easier. The families who disagreed hired an attorney. When the court decided the case had no merit, the group turned to threats. Nothing that could be attributed, of course. And nothing he couldn't handle. And since that type of publicity might harm not only this project, but future business dealings as well, he didn't report the threats to police.

The threats escalated in the weeks prior to the City Council's vote. First, a hateful note slipped under his windshield wiper, promising to research and expose "dark secrets." Second, a copy of a police record charging his mother with drug possession, with a note promising to make the record public. He studied the date. The incident happened prior to her disappearance, when he was just four-years-old. His uncle had probably hired an expensive attorney who got the charges dropped. Third, a break-in through the back door of his home, a modern two-story with floor-to-ceiling glass windows that showcased exceptional views of the pines and waterfront. There was nothing missing or askew in the home, with the exception of a note left on the massive marble island in the rarely-used kitchen: "We can get to you whenever we want."

This last act of intimidation, the day before the Council vote, prompted Rafferty to start using his existing state-of-the-art security system. As time passed without incident, he began to relax.

He understood the desire to protect loved ones, even in death. After all, he had family who resided with the 826 current occupants of Coastal View. Some rested above ground in the mausoleum. But his aunt and uncle had selected standard graves in the open area, although in a prime location near the fountain and rose garden. Their sites were marked by the same unobtrusive ground markers that retained a consistent, pleasant environment in the town's only cemetery.

Chapter 5

Bill Rafferty felt a warmth around the dead. No unpredictable behavior. No senseless rants. No anger. When he searched their faces, he didn't see the sudden, jarring shifts, like an alarm clock sounding unexpectedly. His mother's eyes had clouded; her forehead distorted with wrinkles. Her voice raged louder and louder, drool falling from the corners of her mouth.

At the funeral parlor, his responsibilities grew with each passing birthday. Eventually, his aunt let him assist when she *helped the guests look their best*. The ugly part was done. Blood out; embalming fluid in. Before moving them into their *eternal resting place*, Aunt Jo carefully improved each guest's appearance, so family members retained a positive lasting image of their loved one.

She started with clothing—outfits selected by the spouse, children, or sometimes by the guests themselves in cases of extended illness. Many guests chose formal clothing—suits and even ties for the men; dresses or business pants suits for the ladies; uniforms for police officers, firefighters, military. But slowly the tradition broke. A fisherman in boating attire. A woman in comfortable jeans and college sweatshirt. A young girl in her soccer uniform.

Then there were *meaningful accessories*. Wedding rings. Cross necklace. Bible. Rosary. Family photos. Letters from grandchildren. Paintbrush. Baseball glove. Favorite book of poetry. Harmonica. Bottle of whiskey.

Next came makeup and hair. Jo wasn't certified in either skill, but she had been tutored by professionals and took great pride in her work. The family provided a recent photo, and for a woman, the guest's personal makeup. Jo would finish, compare the photo, then make alterations. Occasionally, she'd be so unhappy with the results, that she'd carefully wipe off all the makeup and start again. For men, she had a small box of products she used to cover any imperfections and leave a glow to the skin.

Jo was especially careful to recreate each guest's hairstyle. For guests who had lost their hair, she visited the wig store two towns over, using a photo to find a close fit. Then she'd get out her shears and hair products to customize.

Bill looked forward to the time he spent with his aunt.

"This is important work, Bill," she said. "The final impression, and they're not able to direct us. All the more reason we must take this seriously."

He was happy to *help the guests look their best*, but happier to be side-by-side with his Aunt Jo. Sometimes he pretended that she was his mother, and more than once, slipped and called her *mom*. She didn't correct him, but he felt strange when he said it, a flutter in his chest. He vowed not to do it again, and then he'd forget.

When he was fifteen, his aunt left, but not the same way as his mother. In fact, everyone already knew she was leaving. At first, Bill tried to pretend otherwise, even when he started to notice things. She forgot that he didn't like raspberries. She forgot to pick him up from piano lessons. She forgot to wake him for school. There were many medical appointments on the calendar, and bottles of pills on the counter. Hospital stays. Whitened skin. Hair on the floor. More and more she resembled the guests.

One day they sat in the living room upstairs. Sometimes the sun hurt his aunt's eyes and she sat in the darkness.

"Should I close the curtains?" he asked. "It's bright today."

"Let's leave them open," she said, with a look that implied she wanted to say more.

Bill sat quietly for a moment, then gave words to what he thought she might be holding back.

"When the time comes," he said slowly. "Do you want me to help you look your best?"

Her eyes fluttered a bit, but she didn't respond. "We could visit the wig shop together," he said. "Or I could go after..."

She reached out and held his hand, then closed her eyes. After a minute, he thought she'd fallen asleep until he saw a drop form in the corner of her eye then roll down her face.

In the end, his aunt must have thought the work too hard for her nephew. When she died, a family friend was asked to help with her hair and makeup, and she looked like Jo again.

On the night before her viewing, Jo was all alone in the main guest parlor. Bill waited until he knew his uncle was in bed, then snuck downstairs to keep her company. At first, he smoothed her dress, adjusted her pearls to place the clasp behind her neck, tucked a stray curl behind her ear, straightened the *Heritage Business Woman of the Year* pin on her sweater, wiped a smudge of pale pink lipstick from above her lip. Then he rested his hand on top of hers for just a moment.

Satisfied that she looked her best, Bill pushed the heavy kneeler aside so he could lie as close as possible to his aunt. He awoke to the sun and the sound of the old gas furnace, clanging off loudly. Whether it was the quiet surroundings or the company of his aunt, he couldn't remember such a sound night's sleep.

Chapter 6

The view would vanish forever. For Loretta, the back waterfront deck was the place she found peace no matter the turmoil. Caring for her mother during an agonizingly slow death from the effects of Alzheimer's. Watching her grandson struggle against the waves of addiction. Grieving the sudden, excruciating loss of grandbaby Sonia. Realizing the effects of stress on her dear Louie's health. Knowing that time was getting shorter.

Maybe it was true that people don't fully appreciate something until it's gone. Or almost gone. Lately, she'd sat outside more often than usual, the windchime's response to the morning breeze a slight, comforting whisper.

Today she had company.

"Iced tea for all," she said, balancing her tray. "And freshly baked apple muffins."

"My Letta's known for her muffins," Lou said to Judy, their realtor.

"Louie gives me too much credit!"

"I'll be the judge of that," Judy said, reaching for a muffin and taking her first bite. She chewed a bit, the couple waiting for her verdict. "Well," she started, swallowing the last bit. "I proclaim Loretta the muffin queen!"

As a sudden breeze hastily clanged the windchimes, Loretta felt the same unsteadiness in her head, wondering if they were making an uncorrectable mistake. Before she could change her mind, she began signing, placing her name next to her husband's by the first X.

She turned the pages quickly, since she'd already reviewed the document last night. After her last signature, she took a deep breath and handed the pen to Judy.

"Our fingers are crossed for a quick sale!" she said although her heart made another wish and she wondered if Louie's did the same. If the wish came true, they'd live in the unsellable house for the rest of their lives, the view reclaimed.

Her heart pulled Loretta toward the house. The familiarity. The warmth the two of them had always known. Still, the logic Lou presented convinced her. Their money would fund three trips a year for the rest of their lives. Four trips if the mutual fund paid off more generously. Loretta and Lou Blake had always wanted to travel. Now in their late sixties, the morning pinch or two in their backs and knees were not-so-subtle reminders. Life had an expiration date.

Before this move, their money was starting to dwindle. Replacement appliances, a new roof, extensive plumbing repairs, and the heartbreaking issues with their grandson kept eating up money they'd worked so hard to set aside.

All of their children were long gone, graduated from college and employed in different parts of the northwest with families of their own. So the Blakes turned to their biggest investment—the house on the water.

Loretta had already started packing for the move, as a way to declutter the home for a quick sale and to ensure they only took what they needed (and wanted) to the much smaller house. She'd given her children a few precious family heirlooms. A small tea set from England, one of the cups chipped by their middle child. The lovely fine-China angel that sat atop their fresh Christmas tree. Two ornate solid wood side tables. A brass-trimmed globe floor lamp from her favorite aunt. At first, Loretta fussed inwardly, wondering if the children would keep those items at all, or if they'd drive directly to the nearest donation drop. Then she wondered why she cared and decided she'd never mention the heirlooms again. They were part of the past. The future would be better.

> *Grow old along with me!*
> *The best is yet to be,*
> *the last of life,*
> *for which the first was made.*

The poem from Browning was a mantra for Loretta now. The contract was signed and all that was left was to wait. Which would prevail, her mind or her heart?

True to the town's real estate trends the Blake's aging home sold not only quickly, but for more than the asking price. Four bidders jumped in with aggressive offers, and in a dazzlingly quick timeframe, the highest was accepted. After settlement, their realtor told them the buyers planned to gut the entire house. The young tech industry couple was looking for a waterfront location, not an old house. Although Lou lamented the loss of the house, Loretta was glad they wouldn't have to see their old life when they drove by.

Moving day came quickly. Unlike their other new Coastal View neighbors who would sleep in a loft, they'd chosen *Tranquility,* the only model with a first-floor bedroom. The once, twice, sometimes three nightly bathroom trips made a loft bedroom impractical, even though they could have opted for actual stairs instead of a ladder. The loft remained and would be a good place for the grandchildren to play when they visited.

The model was under 650 square feet. A retired accountant, Lou loved numbers and the stories they told.

"This house is 4.5 times smaller than the old one," he said, looking up at Loretta from the calculator he'd just unpacked. He clicked a few numbers. "But, now that we're down to a family of two, we'll still have almost as much per person space as we did when we were a family of five."

Loretta nodded, not trusting her voice.

"You won't have as much to clean," he continued.

"I'd have even less to clean if someone would help me," she said, smiling slightly.

Ignoring her, he continued. "And, we didn't have much to move. Here, let me use the box cutter." He stood up from the kitchen chair to break the thick tape on the box labeled "kitchen dishes" that Loretta had on the counter. They both started pulling out and unwrapping the newspaper covered dishes. "These go in the dishwasher first?"

Loretta nodded, feeling a rush of tears starting. "My Louie. As long as we have each other, eh?" She looped her arm under his and pressed into his soft red-flannel shirt.

"Life was pretty sweet at the start, wasn't it? Just the two of us?"

Loretta turned her head so he wouldn't see the tears run down her face.

"Maybe I'll sneak out one night and lop down those pines to see if we have a view," he laughed, hoping to lift her mood.

She shook her head. "Getting us in trouble already, are you?"

"OK my Letta, I suppose our canvas will just have to do. Hey, let's stop for a minute and hang it. Might well make us feel more at home."

How would they compensate for that view? The couple commissioned a local photographer to capture what they saw from inside the old house, then had it printed on a large custom-sized canvas to perfectly fit the wall.

All the front windows of their long-time house overlooked the water, and Loretta's favorite spot in the evening was a small reading nook just off the kitchen with a plump chair, side table to hold her tea, and bookshelf filled from top to bottom with the mysteries she'd bought from the used bookstore and the Rotary Club's annual "fill a bag for

$5" fundraiser. The new place had built-in shelves, and the old chair and side table were positioned adjacent. And now, they hung the canvas where Loretta could see it whenever she glanced up from her reading. It only took her a couple of days to realize this was her new favorite spot.

Lou would miss stepping outside, walking down to his dock, and taking his skiff out for morning fishing, something he did more frequently since retirement. He'd spent 40 years balancing books for marinas, working for a local firm. Lou thought about asking a neighbor if he could move the small boat to their dock, but in the end, he gave it to a young man who worked at one of the marinas, with an agreement that Lou could use it if he had an urge.

For weeks now, the couple tried to push down any residual nostalgic feelings they had about their big home where they'd lived since they married. The place they'd raised their children. If they let themselves, they'd think about their tradition of making homemade pizza after the first day of school, the scent of dough and tomato sauce filling the kitchen. The well-worn farmhouse table where the kids did their homework. The hallway off the side door where backpacks and rain boots were dropped after sloshing through every puddle. The special centerpieces on the dining room table that marked changing seasons and holidays. The indentations on the wood mantel over the fireplace, where stockings were hung with pushpins. The big maple tree on the front lawn where they looped a rope for the tire swing.

Instead, they focused on the house's list of growing negative aspects. The expensive heating bills, the drafty rooms, the high taxes, the dying hot water heater. All the original windows needed to be replaced. These expenses were an uncrossable border, preventing them from trips to Germany, Italy, New York City, Chicago. Besides, the house felt increasingly empty since their last child went off to college.

"I'll be looking forward to getting to know our neighbors better," Lou said. "Imagine they might have reasons of their own for living in such a small place?"

"I expect the cost of the other houses in town," Loretta said. "And 'specially for those just starting out."

"Speaking of other neighbors, when's the special delivery? I could use a bite of something sweet."

"She should be here in an hour. Poor girl. Can't believe Ruth's made to welcome us all, photographer at her side."

"Forgot about the photographer. I best be camera ready," Lou said, patting down his hair and putting on a big smile.

"You're always camera ready, just as you always have something sugary on your mind," Loretta shook her head. "Did the schedule from Bill Rafferty specify a sweet? Could be a cheese and cracker tray for all we know."

"Whatever it is, I hope he's reimbursing her—seems clear it's for publicity."

"Yes, poor dear. Though I'm glad she's finally able to move on. Be more independent," Loretta said. "She was always a quiet thing when I volunteered at the school, but after the fire she drew back even more."

"She seemed excited about the house."

"Now, Louie—when did she tell you that?"

"I talk to people!" he said looking chastised. "She waited on me a couple times at the pharmacy."

"So, we already know Ruth, and then there's Champ of course," Loretta said, remembering weekly tutoring sessions during his elementary school years. "I'm glad we already know a couple of folks. Off to a good start! Now, let's at least get some of this area cleared out for Ruth's visit."

Loretta didn't add that they knew others here in Coastal View. All four of their parents and almost a dozen aunts, uncles, and cousins. And one more resident in a tiny grave. Their granddaughter who died eighteen years ago at just two weeks. Their first grandchild. The four subsequent grandchildren, all boys, brought joy. But she was their only granddaughter. And with her parents living a few hours away now, her grandparents could keep watch over their precious Sonia.

Chapter 7

The same nagging question. Would anyone else look like him? The first time he'd asked himself that question was when he'd left his neighborhood on the outskirts of Philadelphia to accept a full ride from MIT. Would he be the only person of color on his dorm floor? Nearly, with the exception of two Indian roommates down the hall. In his classes? Rarely. At the start-up where he had his first summer internship? Yes.

He was glad his current tech company, Starbyte was more diverse. Although that might not be the same in his new community. He doubted the small number of homes in Coastal View would allow for much diversity. Hopefully, some other singles. Or at least residents his age. Imagine if people thought Coastal View was an over 55 community? Kevin was glad he'd always enjoyed the company of his grandparents.

Since his compressed apartment only held the barest of necessities, the move was easy. All his boxes were inside the new house, and not a single neighbor was in sight. Maybe they were working—a positive sign he wasn't living in a retirement community.

Kevin walked slowly through his new home, then climbed the ladder to the loft and sat on the mattress. Coming from a studio apartment, this place seemed roomy. Once his loveseats were delivered next week he'd have a proper place to sit.

On phone calls with his father and aunt, he talked about his new tiny house, but not the setting. His family would think he was crazy, that he'd lost his mind out here on the west coast.

All the tech companies who made him an offer were in the same general (expensive) region, and choosing Starbyte gave him the advantage of nearby family. His father's first cousin Milt had left Philly and settled in the next town over, moving his landscape business after his wife inherited her grandmother's small retail store. Milt offered a room to Kevin, and he'd almost accepted when he was running out of options.

One of his last options turned out to be a fit for his budget. Kevin considered himself lucky to find a closet-sized studio rental located a reasonable distance from work. He even learned to ignore the alarms from the nearby firehouse that seemed to blare whenever he was drifting off to sleep. He also grew accustomed to the loud commuter train that blew its horn behind his apartment building. It took him a few tries, but he finally found ear plugs that were comfortable enough for sleeping and effective in at least partially muffling the noise.

When he'd imagined buying his first home, Coastal View wasn't what he had in mind. It was logical, though, for several reasons, all which he'd listed on a spreadsheet with relevant data:

- Mortgage and monthly fees lower than apartment

- Walkable to waterfront, services, restaurants

- Bikeable to work

- Quiet

- Large enough to be comfortable

Certainly, it was the perfect size for Kevin and he wasn't expecting many visitors. His father was aging and seemed to be losing motivation for life in general. The decline started after Kevin's mother passed during his last year at MIT. Her death triggered so many changes, especially for his twin sister Kia. She was the last bullet on his Coastal View list:

- More money for Kia

Now Kevin could make his daily commute by bike—in just 35 minutes. His Team Lead agreed to a hybrid schedule, especially fortunate if the snow piled too high for his thin tires to maintain a presence on the asphalt. No need for a car. He'd already found a buyer for his late model Prius. No more monthly payments to Toyota or quarterly car insurance to State Farm. Money for Kia.

The money wouldn't be sent directly to his twin sister. Blind and partially deaf at birth—possibly genetic issues from one of their grandparents--she'd drawn the unlucky gene card. She was also cognitively challenged—not a genetic issue. Kevin was born first. Kia languished. As their mother's blood pressure dropped, there wasn't time for a caesarian section. Only time for the cold hard clamp of forceps against Kia's tiny skull. When her parents counted her fingers and toes, they couldn't help notice the angry, red indentations pressed firmly into both sides of her head.

The hospital never admitted wrongdoing. And prompts by other family members to take the hospital and the doctor to court failed. "She's perfect," was their mother's only response.

Perfect in her mother's eyes. But imperfect in that Kia required a high-level of care. His parents struggled and Kevin did his best to help before he left for college. After his mother died from a massive stroke, his father grew so depressed he forgot to eat or shower. Other family members stepped in to help and were quickly overwhelmed. Nestled away in the academic cocoon of MIT, Kevin didn't realize the severity of the situation. After graduation, he had less than two weeks before his cross country move. His Aunt Diane was spending time with his father every day and had insisted on sending Kia to a facility.

In the middle of his Auntie D's explanation about the move, Kevin asked for the address. He was out the door before she could explain the facility was the best Kia's monthly disability check would cover.

The automatic doors opened. Before he took the first step into the lobby, Kevin breathed in the smell of lemon cleaner, followed by the sour smell of urine. Two elderly, sunken-eyed women sat in wheelchairs near the entrance. The one wearing a crochet gold beanie cap and matching shawl reached out toward him.

"Sir, Sir," she shouted. "I'm hungry and they don't feed us here."

He stopped for a moment, unsure of how to respond when he heard another voice.

"Don't pay the welcoming committee any mind."

He looked in the direction of the new voice. A woman dressed in blue scrubs, adding a paper to the bulletin board next to an unoccupied *Visitors Sign In* window.

"Ida! You know full well we feed you. Leave our guest alone and lower your voice. The whole floor can hear you!"

He gave an awkward nod to the ladies in the wheelchairs as Ida muttered, "Sir, Sir, Sir" on a loop.

The blue scrubs lady turned her attention to him, pointing at the book. "Who're you here to see?"

He printed his name, checked his smart watch (a gift from his corporate recruiter), and added the time in the log book. She led him down the main corridor, took the first right and then the second left. He passed at least a dozen patients in the hall. Most of them with their heads slumped forward like they'd fallen asleep on a long flight. None of them aware of his presence. All of them over 80.

"Here we go," she said, then changed her voice as though talking to a child. "Kia, Kia! Look, look! You have a visitor!"

"She can't see," Kevin said quietly.

"Oh, that's right. She's a special one isn't she?"

Kia was still in bed, but not asleep. Her eyes were open, fixed straight above. As he approached, the floor vibrated slightly, the scent of his aftershave moving toward her. Even before he spoke she knew it was him. Her twin. Kia's face brightened as she propped herself up on her elbows.

"Kev!" she smiled. "My Kev!" He sat beside her on the bed and stroked her cheek. Their signal.

Kevin looked closely at Kia. There was so much about them that was the same. The same thick black hair, both cropped close—his more than Kia's. The same deep-set soft brown eyes. The same even skin tone and dimple on their cheeks. Kia's on her right, and Kevin on his left—like a mirror image. Both were slightly tall, his 6-feet to her 5'8".

Today, her hair was matted, crusts of sleep around her eyes, her nightgown smeared with food stains. The smell of urine. He leaned in, closer to her ear.

"I love you, Kia…"

Another woman in blue scrubs, much younger than the first burst into the room before he could continue.

"The family doesn't usually visit 'til the afternoon," she stammered. "I thought I had more time to get this one up. You can wait outside and I'll move her into her chair. Make her presentable."

"The twins are back together," he said, as Kia smiled.

"Well, at least let me change her diaper," the woman said. "She stinks. Well, they all stink, don't they?"

His eyes still fixed on his twin, Kevin knew what he had to do. In the next three days he toured five facilities. One was a standout. An excellent staff-resident ratio, open visiting hours, on-site physician's assistant, nursing care, physical therapy. There was a daily schedule of therapeutic art sessions and regular appearances by local musicians. On the day Kia moved in, a pianist entertained residents in the gathering room. There was an outdoor garden. Inside, an unmatched attention to cleanliness.

He'd used some of his generous signing bonus to pay his first months' rent. The rest he used to pay Kia's. The facility made transfer arrangements, and she was in her new private room before Kevin had to leave for the west coast. The financial office at Kia's new home helped him set up a direct transfer for the monthly costs not covered by the disability benefit check.

On his previous visit with his father, and out of earshot, his aunt reassured him. "He's improving each day. I think being around people again is helping. And not having to worry about Kia."

His father was sitting on the small screen porch that overlooked the thin cluster of trees on the back end of the property. He was sipping an iced tea and reading the sports section of the *Tribune*. He gave Kevin a long hug before launching into his predictions for the Eagles' season. With the small talk finished his father paused slightly before looking straight at his son.

"Your Auntie D told me what you did for your sister," he said. "She said that place is as nice as a country club. You gave our Kia what I couldn't."

A typically unsentimental man, his father wiped his eyes with the back of his hand, took a long drink of his iced tea, then smiled again.

"We're headed there tomorrow, taking her some of her special things that we were afraid to leave at that first place."

"Ra-Ra?" Kevin asked.

His father laughed. "You know it! Ra-Ra and Kia reunited again."

Early intervention and years of tutoring—all funded by the state of Pennsylvania--had helped Kia make sounds, even some words. Ra-Ra was a silky-soft stuffed rabbit that Kevin bought her after his first paycheck when he was ten years old. He didn't like pulling weeds, but he did like the payoff, so he worked part-time each summer for his Uncle Milt's landscaping company before he relocated the business to the other coast. Kevin graduated from weeds to digging holes, and eventually to mulching and mowing lawns. The hot summer work kept Kevin focused on school. He'd keep his grades up, earn a college degree, and find an indoor job.

"Is this the little guy you're talking about," his aunt said, appearing in the doorway with a brown suede rabbit with a silky white ribbon.

Kevin laughed, "Ra-Ra! She's still holding up, isn't she?"

"Your mother used to wash her by hand," his father said. "She wouldn't even trust the gentle cycle on Ra-Ra. No worries that my favorite shirt once got torn in the machine, Ra-Ra was the *only* thing that got washed by hand."

Somehow his parents managed to give Kevin and Kia a peaceful, loving life. The two of them were able to maintain Kia's care, but he couldn't help but wonder if the years of strain caused his mother's early death. And his father would never be able to maintain Kia's care on his own. There was only Kevin, out on the west coast as far from her as possible.

He'd feel the pull, even from that distance. He felt it most days in college, even when trying to keep his mind focused on his studies. It was still there. He hoped giving her a nice place to live would lessen the pull. Eventually.

Chapter 8

He wanted to live with the dead animals. The area was neglected, overgrown, with barely enough space for a single tiny house lot.

Even after a careful survey to identify all buildable area in Coastal View, Rafferty didn't consider the lot. Too removed from the rest of the community. Who would want to live there? Although now that there was interest, he could charge a premium lot fee. Champ never questioned the extra cost, and neither did his father.

No one ever called Champ by his formal name—Theodore Russell Champion V. His father (Theodore Russell IV) felt pressure from Theodore Russell III to continue the family tradition. When his only son was born slightly premature, he wasn't so sure. The couple's previous two pregnancies had ended in miscarriage. If his son died, the name would die with him. Even if his wife Piper delivered another son, they wouldn't duplicate the name. So they waited until the day he was released from neonatal care, the day their still-fragile son wrapped his tiny hand so securely around Piper's pinky finger that she finally believed he was going to make it.

"What a little champ you are!" she'd exclaimed, then insisted that the baby had tightened his grasp on hearing the word *champ*. And just like other family legends that are rooted by a single incident, that one took permanent hold like the firmness of the baby's grip. The only person who ever called him Theodore Russell or the abbreviated "number 5" was his grandfather.

Champ was often confused, but that didn't have anything to do with his name. His reactions were slower and he seemed to behave differently than others his age, both socially and academically. His parents rallied attention behind him. A string of tutors helped, but didn't heal-- at least in the way they'd expected. A diagnosis of autism left his father depressed about the impact on his son's future, while his mother sought ways to cultivate Champ's passion. His love of animals.

Family trips were planned around opportunities for the young boy to interact with a variety of creatures. There were petting zoos at first, then wildlife sanctuaries for different species—elephants, eagles, foxes. Mother and son volunteered for rescue groups. Before the fire next door, Mr. Sagmire helped Champ make bird feeders to hang around his yard. At first, Champ painted each house the same light blue with navy trim for the door frame. Mr. Sagmire encouraged him to customize each one.

"No two birds are the same," he'd told him. "So maybe birds are drawn to different colors and designs."

Mr. Sagmire used discards from his scrap pile to cut the small wooden sections. Champ would glue them together and once dry, add new colors of paint—light yellow, bright yellow, red. Little Sam started adding simple details—flowers, clouds, hearts. Eventually, the bird feeders filled both the Sagmire and Champion's yards. Piper bought the birdseed and Champ (with Sam's help) took charge of keeping them filled.

After he graduated from high school, Piper steered him to the local community college where (with more tutoring), he completed his studies in Veterinary Technology. There was only one vet in town, but he had a sizeable practice due to the number of local dog and cat owners. Piper was close to the vet's wife, both being members of the Garden Club and the Historic Society, so within a week of graduation and after a cursory interview with the briefest resume review, he was offered a position. The new veterinary tech always worked behind the scenes, the Boxers, Pinchers, Schnauzers, Siamese cats, and the occasional rabbit or guinea pig being nonjudgmental about Champ's lack of social graces.

Mostly, Champ lived a simple life. A slow-moving stream that was rarely, but sometimes, interrupted by unexpected stones tossed in the water.

In elementary school, there had been a few calls from the administrative office. Nothing more than childhood innocence, Piper quickly pointed out to the principal. In one case, Champ disturbed two girls at recess. They were the quietest, most agreeable of girls who were not prone to reporting anything to anyone. A teacher who was reading on the bench while on playground duty heard some sounds that made her think a feral cat had abandoned its litter of kittens. Only the sounds didn't come from kittens. The two little girls crawled on all fours, meowing loudly while Champ patted them on their heads. The teacher reported to the principal that the girls looked quite ill at ease, and when she asked, "You didn't want to crawl around like that, did you?" they said they did not. Further, when the teacher asked them, "So it was Champ who forced you to do this?" they nodded uncomfortably. Subsequent questions and answers revealed that this had gone on all week, and the girls didn't know how to stop the activity. Champ had promised to make collars for the girls out of the ribbon his mother kept in her sewing box.

Piper adopted a cat from the animal rescue group in town, with Champ's agreement that he would never engage in that behavior again.

When Champ was twenty, his father found him outside in the middle of the night watching the neighboring house burn. He held one of the Sagmire family's cats—gray and white with a distinctive black heart-shaped spot on its chest.

Theodore IV and Piper were deeply asleep when the jolting sounds of the fire engines woke them. At the staircase, they saw the open front door. Piper turned quickly to check Champ's bedroom at the end of the hall. He was gone. His father raced outside, with only a terrycloth robe and slippers as a brace against the frigid night air. His mother stayed to check the rest of the house, even though she knew he wasn't there.

At the edge of the woods, he was almost in full shadow, but the reflection from either the fire engine lights or the fire itself hit the top of his head. He wore only his pajamas and socks, so his father slipped his own robe around his son. Champ refused to leave until his father promised they could keep the cat.

For weeks the couple worried (though individually, not together), that someone would ask about the new cat and somehow people would wonder if Champ was connected to the fire. As time went on, they realized worry was needless. This cat (Shadow II) kept to itself. The first Shadow, the rescue cat that had been put down many years ago had been an unusually cuddly cat, always sitting with Champ when they settled down in the evening to watch a movie or play a game of dominoes. Shadow II rarely showed itself and chose instead to spend its time under Champ's bed. Sometimes Champ would try to charm it out from under the bed with a treat or the toy with feathers that the original Shadow had loved. Despite Champ's efforts, he always came downstairs alone, settling next to his mother on the sofa.

"Not tonight. Tomorrow. Tomorrow he will sit on my lap."

And each time, Champ would try just the same, not giving up or even skipping a night. Piper knew the evening routine was fruitless, but she let it go on. *What's a life without hope?* In all things, she tried to teach her son life lessons, no matter how hard—perseverance, free will, disappointment. The lessons were all there. Even if the lessons were painful for him.

They were painful for Piper as well. She felt a little stab in her chest each night when Champ went upstairs, and again when he came down, shaking his head as he sat beside her. He was slowly learning what she already knew. The cat missed its old family and refused to be a part of this new one.

Chapter 9

Evan Bridgeton had roots here, and like other residents, those roots were decaying beneath the surface of Coastal View.

Ten years ago, his newly widowed mother moved her family about eight hours east, to a small farmhouse she'd inherited years before. Previously, she'd rented the home to a young man who worked for a relative's construction company. In exchange for under-market rent, he made some small changes to the home—painting, adding new lighting, repairing the front porch. He always expected the Bridgeton's would sell him the house. When Mrs. Bridgeton called to tell him the lease wouldn't be renewed, he hung up the phone and started considering his options. He only had six weeks.

Evan didn't really know the Sagmires. Neither did his mother or two younger sisters, or even his father. But the connection between the two families was unbreakable.

Mrs. Bridgeton stopped worrying about her husband's occupation years before. No fireman had died or been seriously injured for as long as anyone in town remembered. In the days and weeks that followed, she'd lie awake at night, convinced her lack of worry, her lack of prayers caused his death. She knew she'd never escape those thoughts in Heritage Hill. The overwhelming guilt that swirled around her each night would eventually swallow her, until there was nothing left.

Her kids had one parent left and she couldn't retreat to the growing familiarity of darkness.

The sale of their Heritage Hill home funded a sizeable investment fund. The modest Cape Cod had been passed down from her in-laws, who would have never imagined how much the house would be worth in the future. They could live on her husband's pension and Social Security, with a well-funded money market for the future. After they settled, she'd get a part-time job or work as a substitute teacher.

Evan was 16 when they moved. He didn't want to leave his friends, but was too numb to protest. He missed his old school and his old home most days. He missed his dad every day. Still, his mother looked like she was always on the verge of a disastrous downward fall. Watching her made him think of the once precariously-situated boulder on a hill behind the post office. After an especially turbulent storm started a river of mud, the boulder careened down the hill and into the brick façade, causing extensive damage.

So Evan never protested. He just waited. And while he waited, he thought about the one person who would understand how he felt. He tried to connect with her in the only way he could—by following her on social media. The thought of reaching out to her personally made his mind swirl. Would she blame his father? Think he hadn't done his job properly? Would she see Evan as the lucky one? After all, she'd lost five people, he'd only lost one.

His desire to return home only grew stronger. Every dream for his life started in Heritage. So not long after his high school graduation, arrangements were made. He would move back, live with his aunt and uncle, and work at their marina. His mother was disappointed, but the hardest part was over for her. She'd established friendships, worked at the school, found reasons to be hopeful. She decided her son's move would help him move forward.

Evan never worked, not even part-time during high school. His mother wanted him to focus on his studies and spend time with the few friends he'd made. This first job wasn't easy, but it paid well. His uncle started him with the hardest jobs at the marina, work that had to be completed properly and quickly, no matter the weather. His skin burned under the late summer sun, then prickled and numbed from icy winter winds. There were docks to repair, boats to clean and winterize, equipment to maintain.

His aunt and uncle wouldn't accept rent, and though he insistently paid toward utilities and groceries, he was able to put away much of what he earned. When the first Coastal View press unveiled, his bank account balance showed half the total price—a substantial down payment. He knew straight away the new community was a perfect fit.

Since he'd been back, he'd visited his father's grave on specific dates--his birthday, Father's Day, and the day of the fire. When his mother made her annual visit to see Evan, the two of them visited the grave together. Last year, she oddly decided not to visit the grave. Soon after, one of his sisters mentioned their mother was seeing someone.

Evan wondered if his father felt abandoned. Especially after they all moved. He felt some comfort, and hoped his father did too, that they'd soon be neighbors.

The local paper mentioned that one victim from the tragic fire would be moving to the new community. Evan was thankful the spotlight didn't shine in his direction, but the newspaper was wrong. There were two victims moving to Coastal View.

Chapter 10

These were the new homeowners on Tidings Lane: Ruth, Loretta and Lou, Kevin, Champ, and Evan. Three more *lanes* were already under development, but Tidings was the first. All homes just a few steps away from each other with the exception of Champ's.

Ruth fulfilled her duty, baking a cake for each new resident and delivering it on the day of the move-in. Even though it was Bill Rafferty's suggestion (insistence), Ruth decided the gesture would be a nice way to start. To start a sense of community with her neighbors. Besides, the developer was so excited by the prospect, she couldn't bear to disappoint him, especially since he (or someone he employed) worked so hard to get press—a different publication for each delivery. Today, the photographer from Coastal Living Magazine arrived to snap a few pictures of Ruth spreading strawberry icing on the last cake and delivering it to the last of her new neighbors.

This time she was happy for the company. Champ's house wasn't in view of the other houses, and she remembered the area as overgrown. The photographer accompanied her to the end of Tidings Lane, past the cluster of thick oak trees she had seen years ago when the gate was locked and she was forced to push through the fence.

Champ invited them in, but Ruth declined. She wasn't sure if it was because she wanted to finish the last of her delivery duties quickly, or because of the strange way Champ stared at her chin—or maybe her neck. Ruth self-consciously drew her palm over the area, thinking a dot of stray cake batter may be drawing his attention.

She'd know Champ for years of course, but only on the margins. She often saw him in the workshop, working on the bird feeders. She smiled, remembering how excited Sam was when Champ asked him to add the designs. Remembering how Sam practiced the flowers first on paper to get them just right, then asking Ruth if he'd added the right number of petals, the right color for the center.

With each cake delivery, there was an "after." The time for questions. Unimaginative questions, to which Ruth gave unimaginative answers. Three of the outlets sent a single person as reporter and photographer. This time, the reporter conducted an earlier phone interview. Coastal Living was a thick glossy magazine that she paged through at the library. Fancy houses, designer furniture. She wasn't sure why they were interested in tiny homes and thought they might take a different angle on the interview. Not so. Same unimaginative questions, same unimaginative answers from Ruth. She tried to switch out the descriptors so her quotes were slightly different.

"Does it feel uncomfortable living in a cemetery?"

"It's not uncomfortable. Just different." *Just new. Just unique.*

"What is it about Heritage Hill that makes it such a popular place to live?"

"The lovely waterfront. Small town living." *Beautiful area. Friendly people.*

"Did you move here to be close to your family?" Ruth paused. The others had waited further into the interview to ask this one. "I visited them every week. I already felt close to them."

Ruth knew the reporter would press for more, just like all the others.

"I'm sure. But you're with them every day now. Was that something you considered? Feeling even closer to them?"

"I already felt close to them." Ruth repeated, using the monotone, bored voice she'd perfected during the timeframe that Bill Rafferty termed as *early press interest*. She thought back to the awkward meeting with him, when he gave her a schedule of press interviews.

"I'm not sure I feel comfortable speaking to the press," she'd said quietly, in as humble a way as she knew how.

"But, Ruth! You're the perfect person. The first resident of a whole new concept. Affordable housing in unaffordable markets."

"Can't you do the interviews? You're more experienced and know what to say."

"I have done many interviews, but you're the face of the community. You're speaking for not just your neighbors on Tidings

Lane, not just your future Coastal View neighbors, but for all residents of affordable housing."

She'd accepted the schedule politely. What Rafferty didn't say, but she knew he was thinking, was that Ruth had an obligation. Free housing. She was only required to pay the modest land lease fee of $500 per month, just as all the other residents would do. Although the fee could be raised by 15 percent annually, Rafferty had given his word that the land lease fee would remain unchanged for at least five years. He kept his reason a secret. With so many upcoming projects already in planning, he wouldn't gamble the success of his business against negative press about expensive increases.

She was glad the visits were over now, but surprisingly glad they'd taken place. It gave her a chance to meet Kevin and Evan who were close to her age. She only had a couple of close friends—all female. She hoped the three of them would find enough in common to make a connection. She enjoyed talking with both of them, but was surprised to find her favorite visit was with Loretta and Lou.

Ruth remembered Loretta when she volunteered at the school library, and Lou from his trips to the pharmacy. As a couple, they made a matched set. A smallish version of Mr. and Mrs. Santa Claus. Loretta's tight brown and gray curls framed her round face. Her puffy, rosy cheeks matched those of her husband. His thick gray hair and beard (although both were much shorter than the classic version) completed the illusion. The resemblance to the red-suited couple wasn't just their appearance, but their hospitality as well. She saw Loretta's smile first.

"Well lookie here, Lou! We have our first visitor!"

Loretta pulled the door open the rest of the way, and Ruth saw Lou on the side.

"Oh my—and she has what appears to be a cake," Lou said. "See, Loretta! Ruth knew about my sweet tooth!"

They both moved so Ruth and the reporter/photographer could enter.

"Just a little welcome to the neighborhood," she said. "I don't want to intrude on your time."

"We have nothing but time," Loretta's smile grew. "And how nice to meet our first neighbor! Besides, we need to give you a tour."

"Will take about 30 seconds," Lou laughed.

"I think she knows, Lou. We're all adjusting to the cramped spaces." Loretta frowned slightly, then instantly brightened. Moving here was a practical decision, not an emotional one. And Loretta had learned the hard way she needed to be the couple's practical half.

"Well, now—what about those pills we talked about at the pharmacy?" Lou asked with a wink. "Find any?"

Ruth laughed. "Before you ask," she said, looking at Loretta, "Your husband wondered if we had some miniaturizing pills to reduce all of us, so we could fit more easily into our tiny houses."

Loretta smiled and gave her husband a playful punch in his shoulder.

"It must be a hard adjustment for those of you who lived in big houses," Ruth said. "Since I was just living out of a room at my aunt's house, I'm feeling more stretched out."

"That's a different take on it, for sure," Loretta said, stepping into the living room so Ruth could see the full effect of the upgraded (although undersized) appliances, countertop, and maple cabinets. Loretta had always wanted to replace their dry pine cabinets with maple, but she was too frugal. It seemed top-of-the-line was more achievable on a tiny scale.

Ruth took a polite amount of time to step along the few feet of the kitchen, looking at each feature, including a glass cabinet with an assortment of coffee mugs from different states.

"You must be quite the travelers."

"Not yet," Lou said. "Those were gifts from our family members who continue to be quite the travelers. Now we hope to do the same. See some of those places on the coffee mugs."

"I've never traveled out of the state," Ruth said. "Not once."

"We will have to exchange trip ideas," Loretta said. "I've arranged the mugs to remind us of where we'll go first."

Arizona, New Mexico, and Utah were in view.

"When she's not looking, I change the mugs around, just to tease her," Lou laughed.

Loretta shook her head smiling, then gestured with her hand. "And here's our living room, quaint though it is."

The furniture was more modern than she imagined. Maybe she expected the kind of heavy, old-fashioned upholstered prints in her aunt's sitting room.

Like she was reading her thoughts, Loretta said, "I didn't think our old stuff would fit through that door. We decided to make a fresh start."

There was something in the way she said it that made Ruth wonder if she was talking about more than furniture.

Ruth focused on a large waterfront picture on the wall.

"That was our way of bringing in a touch of the old. The view from our old home. Might be what we'll miss the most."

Ruth nodded, not feeling sure of what to say. The view was spectacular. She'd miss it, too. The second floor of her aunt's house had a large porch with a similar view.

The tour continued. Loretta gestured to the loft, noting it would be a fun place for the grandkids' to play on their visits. Unlike Ruth's home, the back section of the couple's home was expanded with a larger than expected bedroom, the bathroom accessible through a door to the side.

"The loft bedroom would have been a deal breaker," Loretta said. "Lou and I would have broken our necks trying to get up and down that ladder."

Ruth liked her loft. It was cozy, but since it overlooked the downstairs, it didn't feel claustrophobic. She even found herself up there during the day. The ceiling was too low to stand, but she could sit in the little chair from the second-hand shop—a perfect reading nook. The overstuffed chair was comfortable, but the fabric worn and not her style. She planned to re-cover it, if she could find an instructional video for beginners on YouTube.

The tour concluded on the couple's back deck, where there was only room for two Adirondack chairs and a small side table.

"Wish we had a little more space out here, but we can fit more on the grass. Though, everyone will be totin' their own chairs," Loretta laughed. "Storage space won't allow for extra furniture."

When she returned to the house and closed the door, Ruth reflected. All the visits had gone well, even though she had cut Champ's short. Maybe it wasn't the way he stared at her, but the memory of Champ and Sam working together in the backyard. Still, she was glad the publicity was over, even if she'd actually enjoyed her visits.

Much later she'd realize how important those early-seeded friendships would become for the residents of Coastal View—especially Ruth.

Chapter 11

Ruth's customary 5:30 p.m. mailbox visit took just five minutes. and while never excited about the contents of the box, she was comforted by the routine. Work over: 4:30. Home: 5:00. Mailbox: 5:30. The mailperson usually finished earlier, but Ruth cushioned the extra time. Coastal View was the final stop on the route and greetings from the friendly folks of Heritage sometimes slowed the delivery pace. Ruth's father had often stopped his work long enough for a quick chat with their old mailman Randy, now long retired. She wondered what they talked about. Just one more question that would never be answered.

All five mailboxes for the first section were clustered on a single post by the entrance gate. Ruth slipped the key into the lock and turned, then pulled out a stack of what appeared to be mostly advertisements, including one with the headline, *A Clean House is a Happy House*. She laughed to herself. How much effort did it take to clean a tiny house? When she moved the ad to the back of her small stack, she saw something of actual interest--a postcard with a picture of a buffet table set with a wine bottle, glasses, and fruit tray. She flipped it over. In neat, almost machine-like handwriting:

> *You're invited to the*
> *first Coastal View*
> *residents' Happy Hour*
> *Friday, 5 p.m. at Kevin's House,*
> *3 Tidings Lane*

The invitation included a phone number for RSVPs. Ruth heard her heart beating in her ears, maybe a little faster than usual. She tried to decide if she was anxious or excited, and settled on excited. Then the questions started. *What should I wear? What if I don't know what to talk about? What if no one talks to me?* And finally--*What if they ask me about my family?*

Still, it had been ages since she'd been invited to anything that wasn't family or her tiny circle of friends. She walked slowly back to her door, and as she entered, decided to immediately respond before she changed her mind.

The weather was unusually warm for autumn on the day of the party, but had cooled a bit by 5:00. After much deliberation over her three Happy Hour-appropriate outfits, she settled on a simple black pencil skirt paired with a white and black polka-dot sleeveless silk top with a tiny ruffle around the neckline. It was a little dressy, but not overly so. She added a pair of plain black Tom's—her shoe of choice when she wasn't working. She tied her hair back with a clip, but the overall look left the impression of a strict primary school principal, so she let her hair hang loosely. Finally, she settled on her short crystal dangle earrings.

She could see Kevin through the glass door, talking with someone out of view. He smiled broadly as he opened the door for her and moved closer—so much so that she thought he might hug her. Instead, he gestured to welcome her inside where she saw the previously unseen guest—Evan, whose face seemed to brighten (was that her imagination?) as he reached out and shook her hand.

"Nice to see you again, Ruth."

"This might be it," Kevin said. "Just us three. Loretta and Lou send their best, but you may have noticed they are traveling this week. And I didn't hear from Champ."

His face froze slightly after saying the name, and in fact, all three faces froze slightly, like there was something more to be said, but instead they were silent.

Ruth glanced around. "You've done such a nice job here. Really came together."

When she'd made her cake delivery, Kevin had been surrounded by boxes.

"I still have a few boxes up in the loft. Thought I'd give the appearance that I was actually organized," he laughed. "I'm glad the loveseats were delivered--otherwise we'd be sitting on pillows."

Evan smiled. "There's a reason I'm not hosting anything at my place. Mostly because my unpacked boxes are on top of my sofa."

Ruth returned his smile, sympathetically. When she'd delivered Evan's cake, he stood uncomfortably near the door. She felt surprisingly relieved that it wasn't because of Ruth herself.

"How about you, Ruth?" Kevin asked. "Are you still unpacking? All settled?"

"I'm settled. Maybe it was easier for me because I didn't have much to begin with. I wasn't living on my own yet so I'd only purchased what I needed right away."

Ruth glanced at the counter with two bottles of wine and an empty wine glass, and Kevin noticed.

"What can I get you, Ruth? White or red? I also have some beer in the fridge, some sparkling water, ginger ale."

"I'll try a glass of the white," Ruth said, making a mental note to keep it at one. She wasn't much of a drinker and didn't want to make a poor impression. Or start reciting her life story.

Once Ruth had her drink in hand, Kevin gestured to the living space. "Let's have a seat." There were two loveseats and a coffee table that Ruth knew could be configured into a bed for guests. There was only one local furniture store, and the salesman had mentioned the set worked well in tiny houses. Ruth had the same set, although Kevin's a medium gray and Ruth's white. Aunt Indy thought white wasn't practical, but since there wasn't a pet or a child in the home, Ruth figured she'd manage to keep it clean. She slid to the wall on one side, Evan to the other loveseat, and Kevin took the spot beside her then popped right back up.

"Let me get a tray into the oven," he said.

Ruth took a sip of wine and when she looked up at Evan was smiling at her. "Did people think it odd when you told them about Coastal View? I mean that you were going to live here?"

She laughed. "The short answer? Yes. Actually, everyone thought it was odd with the exception of one of my customers, Mrs. Bentley. She's a sweet old lady—always smiling. She told me 'My Henry will keep watch over you'."

"Oh! Her deceased husband, I take it?"

Ruth nodded. "She also assured me I wouldn't have noisy neighbors."

"Definitely a plus," Kevin said, returning to the table with a meat, cheese, and cracker board and little napkins. "Please help yourself. I have some more substantial appetizers in the oven."

"Did you have noisy neighbors before?" Ruth asked Kevin.

"I had the noisiest neighbor of all, especially at night. The commuter trains. I finally tuned it out, but I'm not sure I got much sleep my first month. And there was the added bonus of the rare, but occasional firehouse alarm."

"Did you live there long?" Evan asked.

"Since I relocated a year ago—from back East."

Kevin took a long drink from his wine glass, waiting for the next question.

"Assume you relocated for work?" Evan continued.

"Yes—finished school and made the move to the land of tech," he said, looking at Evan. "How about you? From this area? Transplant?"

"From here originally, moved back. My aunt and uncle needed some help with their business—they own that big marina on the waterfront. Seemed like a good time to move back. I missed it."

Ruth thought Evan looked uncomfortable, but maybe her feelings were based on her own discomfort. She wasn't anxious to share her background, even though most of it was well-known with the recent newspaper coverage. Still, she decided to go on the offense.

"Living here all my life, I probably take this place for granted," she said. "What did you miss most?"

Evan paused and Ruth thought she saw a look she could only describe as regret pass across his face. "The harbor, the water. I can't imagine there's anyplace this beautiful, though I haven't traveled much."

"And you, Kevin? What do you like most about the area?" Ruth asked.

"It's interesting here. On the one hand, we're living in these tiny houses because there's such limited living space. But when you're outdoors, there's a sense of vastness. Does that make sense? And, I agree with you Evan about the waterfront. I'm lucky to have that view when I bike to work. Couldn't do that on the east coast—the only safe bike lanes where I grew up were in state parks."

"How 'bout you Ruth?" Evan asked.

Ruth weighed her answers. She could be funny (and truthful) and say *I don't know any better—I've never lived anywhere else*. She could be even more honest and say—*I'd feel guilty to leave my family behind*. Or she could stick with the expected.

"What's not to like? I suppose it's really the waterfront—I love spending time at the beach. And the trees. It's quiet as well. I suppose we're the lucky ones to find an affordable option in a town where other people pay millions of dollars."

Ruth felt herself blush a little, since she knew her luck (or misfortune) meant her home was the most affordable of all. She commented on the wine instead, which led to a discussion on the new wine and small plates restaurant next to the marina.

The oven timer dinged and Kevin made small talk from the kitchen (just a couple feet away) until he returned with the appetizers. He described each one as his guests nodded enthusiastically. Before long, there was only a single crab-stuffed mushroom cap left on the tray and he asked if anyone needed a refill. The time had flowed easily—as the three exchanged information on their favorite local places, rumors of businesses coming to the area, the lack of new bestsellers at the library, and the next phase of building at Coastal View. Ruth had stayed longer than she planned and thought this was a smooth time to exit.

"This was so nice…so nice of you to host Kevin, but it's time for me to go."

Evan frowned, but slid out from his seat as well. "Same for me. Don't want to be one of those guests who never leave."

Kevin stiffly offered both his guests a handshake and took exactly seven steps to open the door.

As they walked down the porch stairs and heard Kevin shut the door, Evan turned to face Ruth. "Any interest in grabbing a cup of coffee tomorrow morning?"

Two days after the Happy Hour, Kevin absently sorted through mail when he saw Champ's RSVP—he'd written NO in large block letters on the invitation and had slipped it into Kevin's mailbox slot.

73

Chapter 12

The task was slower when the ground was hard. Cool weather and no rain for weeks. A shallower grave would do, though he hated changing the plan. He reminded himself, as he always did, that life-long criminals were successful as long as they followed their plans. With deviation, even small, they risked getting caught. He hated the comparison though, because his efforts were not criminal, not self-serving. His efforts were meant to help.

Thinking again about the importance of his mission made him dig harder, faster. Finally out of breath, he decided the grave could be less shallow. *An improvement on the original plan.*

What he didn't know, on that crisp late autumn night was that this girl was different. Most had already been abandoned, or at least their disappearance wouldn't cause a major search. He confirmed that when he spoke with them, drawing them into his confidence. No one would be looking for them, or at least they wouldn't look here.

Before he could verify, she resisted. And when she resisted he became irritated, then angry, and finally outraged. After all, he was just trying to help her.

Soon he would learn that his efforts to follow his plan had failed. Not because of the rush to finish the grave. Not because of the depth.

This time the girl wasn't like the rest. This time people were looking for her. And this time they wouldn't give up. And despite all of his efforts, there was only so much he could do to stop them.

Chapter 13

Bill Rafferty knew publicity would wane. He just didn't expect it so soon. His big picture strategy relied on the next section of Coastal View. He was realistic from the start, knowing the second section wouldn't generate as much publicity as the first. Yet even those realistic, diminished expectations proved optimistic. The first angle had been tantalizing, completely unexpected. Like a magic beanstalk stretching into the clouds. And even though section two meant an even taller beanstalk, no one was interested.

Section B would be four times the size of the premier, Section A. At the Open House unveiling, hopeful buyers added their names to a waiting list, not realizing the cost would increase by 18%. Still, Rafferty hoped continuing buzz about the project would not only sell out B immediately, but would start setting the stage for the most lucrative part of the overall plan. Franchises for cemetery owners.

Lack of publicity was only the first challenge. The second, a missing indigenous girl from Canada. She was last seen on the security camera focused near the Coastal View entrance. Rafferty added the camera to impress potential buyers with the extra measure of safety. Now it might put his well-reasoned plan at risk.

Canadian authorities had traced fifteen-year-old Vista across the border. A couple reported seeing her hitchhiking on a highway about 10 miles north of town.

U.S. law enforcement went to extra lengths, maybe due to prior controversy about the lack of U.S. cooperation in these kinds of cases. Maybe because Vista had family in law enforcement on both sides of the border. Or maybe because cable news was running the story nonstop.

Security video showed the teen walking by the gas station, post office, and through the small "downtown" region and marina district as she passed the waterfront park, three restaurants, a coffee shop, and a hardware store. The last camera that captured her image was outside Coastal View.

Rafferty was prepared if the question about safety emerged. He hired semi-retired Deputy Sheriff Jack Granston to patrol Coastal View. The arrangement called for him to patrol the perimeter in his vehicle and walk the grounds four times a week—at varied times. And if Deputy Sheriff Granston wanted to breeze by the entrance in his patrol car during his working hours, well that would certainly be an added bonus.

So far, the exact location of the final security camera wasn't disclosed to the media, likely due to Rafferty's cultivated relationship with local law enforcement. He wanted publicity. Just not that kind of publicity.

It wasn't like this was the first girl who disappeared along the Pacific Northwest coast. These disappearances started further north, girls from rural U.S. or Canadian towns searching for a way out. Some were just looking for safety. Protection from the men they knew, like their stepbrothers, uncles, teachers. And protection from those they barely knew. There was a culture of silence in many of these communities—no expectation anyone would believe them or even listen.

Girls who saw their friends and classmates run away believed something positive had happened. They'd made it down the coast and were living a glamorous life--modeling, dating a rich actor, earning big tips at an oceanfront bar in LA. If the girls couldn't be found, it was because they were clever. They'd hidden their tracks wisely and were happy in their new lives.

That was the furthest their friends' imaginations would stretch. In most cases, their families didn't expect their girls would be found, so they also believed the stories, the fables that circulated. They had to.

Although most people had never heard of the many girls who'd taken the same heartbreaking path, Vista had the kind of resume the media loved. She played ice hockey. She participated in heritage days. She volunteered with her friends at the animal shelter. She was pretty. Vista's mother wanted the press to know her daughter. She sent out a mass of photos and the cable news stations flashed them on the screen. Taking a shot on the ice. Holding a tiny puppy on her lap, the rest of the litter around her. Selfies at the park, coffee shop, a school dance. Short videos of her laughing, blowing out birthday candles, skipping down the sidewalk. The pictures said what the commentators did not: *She could be your daughter, your sister, your niece.*

In Coastal View, the Deputy Sheriff would visit each home personally, wearing his uniform so there wasn't any question about his intentions. Bill Rafferty made it clear--the safety of all residents rested firmly on Granston's shoulders.

Chapter 14

On the third Saturday in October, Granston started at the furthest house. The one set apart from the others. As he knocked on the door, he saw Champ fold back one of the front window shutters. He turned and nodded, but Champ frowned, staring for what seemed to the Deputy like five minutes, but probably closer to five seconds. Next, he folded the shutter back over the window, then slowly opened the door, still frowning.

"Theodore Champion?" he asked, putting out his hand.

Champ kept his hands on the side of the door. "I didn't do anything," he said in a voice that was louder than necessary. "Why are you here?"

Granston put his hand down and tried a stiff smile. "No sir, you certainly didn't do anything. I'm just here to introduce myself."

He shifted uneasily to his other foot, waiting for a response. Champ's frown seemed permanent. Granston shifted to professional mode.

"I was hired to provide security to the residents of Coastal View. It's a safe and peaceful place, and Mr. Rafferty wants it to stay that way," he said, following the script his boss provided. "You might see me driving or walking through a few times a week. If you have any questions or concerns, feel free to contact me anytime."

He reached into his front pocket, pulled out a business card, and held it toward the door. Champ waited a few seconds, a game of chicken between the two. And just as Granston thought about placing the card on the floor of the small deck in front of the door, Champ reached out, snapped the edge of the card, pulled it back and closed the door. He repeated his earlier process and opened the shutter. Watching. Frowning.

Granston looked directly at him before returning to his car. He wondered if the rest of Coastal View knew what an odd little man lived in their midst. Maybe more than odd. Granston decided it would be smart to let the other residents know his feelings about Champ once he'd gained the others' trust. In the meantime, he'd see what he could find out about him. He vaguely knew the family. Big money. But every family had their secrets, didn't they? Their own shame.

He put the first visit out of his mind to prepare for the second. Another family with a secret. As he knocked on the door, he wondered if Loretta and Lou would remember him. It had been a couple of years, but when you took out a restraining order on your own grandson, the humiliation wouldn't fade easily.

The visit only lasted five minutes or so, and if the couple remembered Granston, they showed no signs. Maybe they'd blocked out that time in their lives. Or maybe they were hoping the Deputy

Sheriff had forgotten and wouldn't raise the subject with their neighbors. The last update Granston heard about the grandson, he was in a well-respected rehab specializing in opioid addiction.

Three more stops to go. In and out quickly at each, but he'd found himself wanting to linger at Ruth's house. The young woman was thoughtful, offered him a glass of iced tea or hot coffee (he accepted the first). Of course he knew her story—everyone did. She was a sweet young woman, one that the whole town wished the best. He had his misgivings about Coastal View and Bill Rafferty in general, but the fact that the first house went to Ruth—that was something good.

Crime was still low in town. An occasional defacing of a wall with graffiti, an even more occasional small ticket item stolen from an unlocked car. Crime would be even lower, non-existent in Coastal View on Granston's watch. Although no one could have predicted that this safe place might have a decidedly unsafe neighbor. But, he reminded himself, that's why he was here. To take care of people who didn't even know they were in danger.

Chapter 15

They'd never agreed, or even discussed. Yet somehow Ruth and Evan independently decided to keep their relationship quiet. Away from any prying eyes in the neighborhood, although there was only a total of six eyes—two each belonging to their neighbors. Eight eyes if they included Champ, which they rarely did.

The fact was that everyone, including Champ, was well aware the couple was dating.

Ruth and Evan had a routine now, meeting in town twice a week after work for a drink and dinner. They returned to Coastal View together, although it was dark or nearly dark each time. Now a month after Kevin's Happy Hour the couple had been together exactly eight times. In Ruth's view—just right. In Evan's—too few. He could feel Ruth's desire to take things slow. Once, when Evan wondered if they might meet at the movie theater the next day, Ruth hesitated before saying the next day wouldn't work for her. So Evan planned to maintain two dates a week, until he sensed Ruth's comfort with a third.

Kirby's Pub was nearly empty when Evan arrived. He liked to be there first, facing the door in the small booth at the end of the bar area. When Ruth entered, she looked straight over and smiled, her face framed by the faux black fur around the hood of her black puffer jacket. She stamped wet snow off her boots at the entrance, pulling her hood back and unzipping her jacket.

Evan smiled back. Recently, he realized he involuntarily smiled every time he thought of her.

"Snowing hard?" he asked as she slipped off her coat and put it on the hook. "Steady," she said. "Feels like a thick snow…wet."

"Seems early, doesn't it?"

"Probably. Though I'm always surprised by the first one."

"About to get 30 hours of it last heard," he said as Ruth slid across from him. "The first and also a substantial one."

"Makes it all so quiet, doesn't it?"

Before he could answer their usual waitress, Daria was at the table.

"The red blend?" she asked.

Ruth nodded. "Yes, please."

"Dinner or just appetizers?" she asked.

"Dinner," they both said at once, then laughed.

Daria left menus on the end of the table before leaving.

"We may not make it out tomorrow," Evan said. "With the snow and all."

"Lucky it's a Friday," Ruth said. "The pharmacy is open on Saturday, but just for a few hours. I rarely work on the weekend—including tomorrow. You?"

"I finished up the work at the marina today—went in earlier than usual. I don't mind a good walk in the snow, but I wanted the option of staying in."

"Binge-watching plans?"

Evan laughed. "I've shared too much about myself already! Now you think I'm sitting on the couch every weekend with a six-pack!"

"Well, I suppose I wouldn't blame you. Not like tidying up the house takes much time. I have my version of binge-watching ready. Three books I've been wanting to read, one due back at the library next week."

"Do they really charge a fee if you're late?"

"Hmmm. Well, can't remember being late! I do like to follow the rules. Now I'm giving you too much information about myself!"

Daria dropped the wine off and glanced at the untouched menus. "I'll check back later."

"To binge-watching," Evan said raising his beer to toast with Ruth.

"And binge reading," she laughed.

"Our lazy habits seem like less-personal sharing, don't you think?" Evan asked, as Ruth took another sip from her glass, hoping this wasn't transitioning to a deeper discussion. The door opened as three men tumbled in, the wind drafting across their booth and Ruth shivered.

"I'm not sure if you know...you probably don't," Evan continued slowly. "But we have a connection. A tragic one, actually."

Ruth looked up from her glass, her brow wrinkled. Evan's face was slightly flushed, his eyes narrowed. He looked back down at the table.

"I've been wanting to mention, but it's just…It's the fire. You weren't the only one to lose family that day. I'm sure you read about it. About my connection."

Ruth stared back, trying to imagine what Evan might mean. She'd never read anything about the fire. It was a subject she'd avoided. With the exception of the first year after and the recent publicity, no one, including her aunt, cousins, and friends, ever talked to her about the fire. Like they all understood the subject was taboo.

"My family, my father," Evan continued, looking back at Ruth.

Ruth studied Evan, his eyes now filling with tears, and she could feel her own do the same. How could this be? Why didn't she know there was another family affected by the fire? How was that even possible?

Evan was still looking at her, waiting for a response. "I don't understand," Ruth said, shaking her head.

"My father…he was a fireman. His truck was the first to respond."

Ruth failed to stifle a gasp. "I'm so sorry, Evan. I had no idea." She wiped under both eyes with the backs of her hands. "Truly sorry."

"I never meant to upset you, Ruth," he said. "I'm the one who's sorry for mentioning. I should have realized it's still so painful."

But there it was. Another life lost because of her. Ruth reached out her hand to hold Evan's, a gesture of apology that he would only see as kindness.

"My family moved away afterwards," he said. "It was just too hard for my mother. All the memories of him. Did you ever think about leaving, Ruth?"

She took a moment to consider her answer first. She couldn't tell Evan that she needed to stay here, to atone. A kind of penance that ensured she'd be here forever. Until she finally rested beside her family.

"That really wasn't an option for me. My aunt and her family—they were all I had," Ruth said, realizing she was telling the truth, or at least part of the truth. "I supposed I could have gone off to college, but four years seemed like such a commitment, or maybe too much of a change."

"That makes sense. I didn't have an option either. My mother made the decision. I made the best of it, but I never wanted to leave. If losing my father was hard for me, it was even harder for her," he said, pausing to take a sip. "I didn't want to make life any harder for my mom, so I told myself I'd find a way to get back here when I was old enough."

Ruth nodded, hoping he wouldn't press for more. Maybe now that he'd said what he needed to say, what he'd probably been waiting to say since he met her, that would be the end of it. She'd grown really fond of their time together, but there was only so much she could, or would reveal. And now Evan was one more person who would never know the full truth. Ruth would take her secret to the grave.

Chapter 16

Granston took his new part-time job seriously. By his measure, two part-time jobs didn't equal full-time stress. Especially full-time work in the Sherriff's Department. A year ago, he'd retired. With recruitments down, they'd hired him back part-time. A kinder, gentler position. No more late nights completing personnel paperwork. No more closed-door sessions with subordinates. Plus, the money was good. Collecting his retirement pension and now earning his pre-retirement hourly rate. Then there was the new, even higher paying part-time job. Maybe he'd finally buy a hunting cabin in the woods up north. What good was the money if he didn't enjoy it?

Granston lived just inside the Heritage Hill zone, in a small apartment turned condo passed down from his mother. Incredibly well priced for the zip code, but still out of reach for most.

He started strong at Coastal View, patrolling the area in his private car (discretion!) at both regular and irregular times. He walked the perimeter, checking for loose spots in the fence.

There was a resident's parking pad out-of-view behind the imposing-looking mausoleum building. When he walked through, he noted the name "Champion" inscribed on three of the markers. One who was already gone (clearly Champ's mother) and two more spaces with names and "born in" dates. Granston wondered how it felt for Champ and his father to visit and see their future hotel. And it did resemble a hotel. There was even a chandelier in the center, with thickly upholstered benches and marble floor tiles so clean it looked like no one had set foot on them. The heels of his shoes echoed with each step. He wondered how much each deluxe accommodation cost. More than the tiny houses? Definitely, especially based on the names he saw on the markers. The town's wealthiest old-moneyed families. Not a place Granston could afford. When his sister died unexpectedly, his mother cremated her body. The only affordable option, and one his mother had insisted on for herself as well. He wondered if Ruth's family had been reduced to ashes in the fire. Maybe they had that in common.

On his first two parking pad visits, there was only one vehicle parked there—Lou and Loretta's truck. Last Saturday, there were two more—both SUVs with school stickers on the back. When he'd driven down Tidings Lane, he saw people outside the couple's home—the vehicles must belong to their children.

He'd already checked public records on all the residents. Nothing of note on Ruth, Kevin, or Evan. He already knew about the restraining order issued by Loretta and Lou on their grandson Michael, and reports about two break-ins at their waterfront home. Lou was the one who reported the robberies (some cash they kept at the house) and Loretta seemed unhappy her husband had reported the crimes at all. Granston noted that both the crimes happened just a few months before the restraining order.

There were a few complaints about Champ that never amounted to anything. He was a suspect in the disappearance of a German Shepherd who lived two houses away. The owners, a sitting judge and his wife, were certain Champ had taken the dog, given his overzealous fascination with their pet. The dog was more like a son to the couple, and they were vocal and persistent in their suspicions.

But that spring when the pond near their house unthawed, the body of their precious pet floated to the surface. It was assumed that the dog (they admitted he loved to slide on the ice) had broken through a thin spot. There was a heavy snow storm the night he disappeared, which likely covered and re-froze the spot where he slipped through the surface. A neighborhood child, on a walk with her mother around the lake, was the first to spot the brown fur. The mother thought it was a coat, or even an unfortunate groundhog until moving a little closer. She quickly turned away with her daughter, realizing it was the missing dog.

One minute the mother and daughter were looking for daffodils pushing up through the recently frozen ground. The next staring at a beloved pet, its fur strangely preserved from the cold.

As Granston pulled up the local area map, he noticed something else. Champ and his parents lived beside the Sagmire family. The place where Ruth's family had died. There was a thickly wooded section between the homes, which couldn't have been more different: the Sagmires living a very rural existence and the

Champions living in luxury. He reminded himself to look into the details of the fire.

When Granston visited the residences, he checked the locks on the front doors--builder-grade single locks. The back doors were probably the same. He made an appointment with the owner of the local hardware store to find out the best options for upgrades. He figured most people preferred a single key for all their locks—less to remember. Replacing the front and back locks and adding a deadbolt to at least the front door, all using the same key, would be appealing to the residents. Maybe he'd convince Rafferty to cover a part of the cost, especially in light of the missing girl.

Granston stayed closely connected to the investigation of the Canadian girl's disappearance. There was a witness who claimed they saw her hitchhiking south of town, which could divert attention from Heritage. Maybe media attention would shift down to LA, already a popular destination for runaways. A city that held every promise. Granston knew that was merely a fable. Instead, innocent girls found themselves in a dark place living an ugly life.

He decided to compile a list of trucking companies that made runs between the last place the girl was spotted to the hitchhiking location. He'd flag the routes that continued down to LA. There'd be a lot of research required to check out each driver, but at least his list would set them off in the right direction—away from Coastal View.

At this next appointment with Bill Rafferty, he'd provide some information on the locks and the latest on the investigation. At their prior meeting, Granston said the introductory visits had gone well, but kept his feelings about Champ to himself. He would also keep his research into Champ's background and the location of his family house close hold. There was only so much Rafferty needed to know for now.

Chapter 17

The wreaths were lit on the front gates of Coastal View. A signal that visitors would increase between the hours 9 and 4. Loved ones maintained set routines for gravesite calls. Bouquets fashioned with sprigs of holly and pine in the pewter vases. Small, usually unadorned Christmas trees. An occasional stuffed bear with a big red ribbon from those who'd lost a young child.

She tried not to look at the stuffed animals, although she saw Loretta place a stuffed *something* on a grave a few rows away. Child? Grandchild? Ruth certainly wouldn't be so insensitive to ask.

This time of year made her especially tenderhearted. She was sad for those families. Sad for herself. Sad for her younger siblings, especially Sam. She never left a bear on his grave. It would only make her cry. And what would she do with it when the winter ice and snow covered it? She couldn't imagine throwing it away, although the maintenance crew would certainly dispose of it after the holiday.

Instead she left a Christmas bouquet in each vase. She'd long perfected them over the years using wide, red velvet ribbon that she'd bought at the local craft store. There were evergreens that bordered the entire back fence of Coastal View. This year as she walked along the inside of the fence snipping off sprigs, she noticed one of the graves on the edge of the pet section had been disturbed —probably by prospective homeowners checking out the area. She'd never seen anyone back there. Maybe pet owners didn't actually visit graves. Maybe it was enough to know the family dog or cat had a peaceful resting place.

Unless she was mistaken, the blueprints Bill Rafferty displayed with future development indicated the pet section was filled and closed.

Tiny house construction continued. If people didn't typically buy houses in the winter, especially before the holidays, that wasn't the case here. Although, Coastal View wasn't part of the typical housing market.

Ruth wondered if Rafferty's idea was to increase sales by decreasing available inventory. If so, he was successful. Anyone interested in minimalism, a low carbon footprint, reasonable prices, a sense of community, or any combination of those factors was waiting to move here. Each new release was an opportunity to raise prices. Yet interest never slowed. From what she'd heard about the overall Heritage market, Coastal View's new price increases were incredibly modest in comparison.

While Ruth was chatting at the mailbox with Lou recently, he mentioned those seemingly modest increases.

"Do you think anyone checked the numbers based on square feet," he said, shaking his head. "I did. Not much of a bargain at all."

"Doesn't seem like anyone cares," Ruth laughed, motioning toward the newly framed houses.

"They're looking at the rest of Heritage. Got to compare apples to apples."

"I suppose it's good we got in when we did."

If Ruth had waited for the second round, Rafferty wouldn't have needed the publicity, and she wouldn't be living here.

So even on a cold December Saturday afternoon, as Ruth adjusted the soft red velvet bows and arranged the simple bouquets in five vases, she heard the echo of hammers. She saw a future homeowner peering first at her, then over her head to see the four tiny houses in view on Tidings Lane. Combined with the holiday grave visitors, Coastal View was crowded. For people who expected this new community to be peaceful and quiet during the Christmas season, it was not. At least, not until later in the day when the front gate was locked and only current residents had the code to enter.

Ruth couldn't help but compare this new Coastal View to the Coastal View she'd known for years. Before, she could hear her own breath as she knelt at the graves. Although recently, she'd abandoned her long-established practice of kneeling. She felt self-conscious with so many people around.

The last thing Ruth ever wanted was for people to feel sorry for her. She didn't deserve it. She'd known that since the first moments after learning her family died in the fire. Now she knew it even more, considering that another family had suffered because of her.

Evan seemed more interested in her than ever, which only increased her anxiety. Over the years, she'd learned to push the anxiety down, to say a prayer, to visualize something happy. She didn't want to end her time with Evan. She liked talking with him at the coffee shop, or the diner, or the little bar down near the marina. She loved the way he tilted his head back and to the right when he laughed. How he closed his eyes to remember a detail when he told a story. How he ordered her red blend wine and had it waiting before she arrived and then stood to give her a hug before she sat down. Sometimes she was successful in forgetting about what happened, about what she cost him.

She'd keep trying to close that door. The past was the past. It was over and there was nothing she could do about it. She liked to think that Evan was as happy spending time with her as she was spending time with him. Breaking it off would just hurt him further. So maybe by moving forward with Evan, she'd found a way to redemption. And she'd never want to cause him any more pain by telling him.

All couples had their secrets, didn't they?

Chapter 18

Christmas was just a week away. The residents were sharing their plans—some going away, others staying home for the holidays. Even building ceased. No sound of hammering, no builder pick-up trucks blocking lanes.

Kevin was flying east in a few days and asked the others to keep an eye on his place. Granston had replaced the locks, which gave him, and the rest of the residents, an increased sense of security. Not that any of them ever felt unsafe.

Loretta and Lou had warned their neighbors about an influx of family on Christmas Eve. After lunch in the cramped quarters, the couple would join their family at a large historic resort just east of town. Their children had booked rooms for a couple of nights and reserved one of the smaller banquet halls. The hotel had set up a visit from Santa and full Christmas dinner. This would be the first holiday away from their longtime home, and they were determined to make it as lovely and memorable as possible.

Ruth would spend Christmas with her aunt and family. The grandchildren would be in a frenzied state by the time she made the walk from her new home to her old home.

Since her family's deaths, she'd spent every Christmas at her aunt's house. This year there would be a slight deviation from the tradition. Snow predictions changed Evan's plans to spend Christmas with his mother and siblings. He'd planned to borrow his uncle's truck and spend four days there. Instead, he'd spend the day with his aunt and uncle, and make the trip out of state when the forecast looked stable.

He'd invited Ruth to join him on Christmas afternoon. When she explained her own tradition, that included a late lunch with her extended family, Evan persisted, suggesting she could join them for dinner or just dessert. Ruth surprised herself when she agreed, and was especially pleased to see Evan's reaction—his eyes and whole face brightened.

Then he mentioned that Santa would certainly have something under the tree with her name. Ruth appreciated his comment, because she hadn't considered buying something for him, thinking he'd be away.

Ruth had already bought and wrapped her gifts for family, consulting with her aunt about the grandchildren's ages, likes, and dislikes. As was her custom, she'd bought books for everyone. Since her aunt spent her time trying out new recipes or watching PBS travel shows, she'd long ago settled on cookbooks, ones tied to particular regions of the world. She felt especially glad to find a new volume by one of her aunt's favorite chefs that featured soups from northern Europe. She'd paired the book with a new emerald green apron with a ruffle at the top and bottom that gave it a retro, old-fashioned look. There was a secondary benefit to her gift. Ruth was hoping to learn a few more signature dishes, and her aunt would certainly try out a few of the soups during the year, and (at Ruth's request) write out the recipes on index cards in her perfect cursive penmanship.

For her cousins, Martha and Lenora, she bought recently released novels from each of their favorite authors. For the others, her frequent trips to the back section of the bookstore had paid off. She found a used, but pristine copy of a highly-recommended book of essays about the Civil War for Martha's husband. He frequently lamented that the only television worth watching were shows on The History Channel. Lenora's husband was an avid reader, so she bought him the latest Amor Towles' novel. Ruth also found used, clean copies of picture and chapter books for the grandchildren. It always amazed her why people would spend more for a new book when the used book was so well kept. Even still, Ruth rarely splurged on even a used book—the local library was well-stocked, even if recent bestsellers were slow to the shelves.

Now she could turn her attention to a gift for Evan. Something thoughtful. She ran through their conversations. What did he like? His descriptions of Netflix series leaned toward crime fiction, with an occasional shift to a real crime docuseries. The fiction series he'd talked about the most was Longmire, and a Google search for "books for fans of Longmire" provided a list of books on which the show was based.

He'd also talked about coffee more than most people, animatedly describing the coffee's two distinct seasons—hot and iced. She'd learned that while he was satisfied with the hot coffee he'd brewed at home, he still hadn't learned the right formula for brewing iced coffee for the summer. One of her coworkers Justin drank iced coffee year-round, so Ruth asked him if there was some special blend he used.

"The secret is a coffee press," he said. "You can get the coffee ground differently, but the press is non-negotiable."

"Are they expensive?"

Justin was already searching his phone. "Look—they start at $20 and go up from there," he said, eyes fixed as he scrolled. "This one —$35 and some change. I know this brand and they make solid stuff. I'll text you the link."

Ruth ordered the press right after work, checking first to ensure it would arrive in plenty of time before Christmas. She stopped by the coffee shop after, asking for a recommended iced coffee blend, and whether it would remain fresh enough after the first thaw.

She left with a one-pound bag, then headed for the bookstore. One of the five books from the Longmire list was available, but not in the used section. She didn't mind paying a little more for something she was sure Evan would enjoy.

As she headed back to Coastal View she thought about a card. The hardest decision of all. She'd bought one box of cards with glittery green Christmas trees on the front to give to her aunt and cousins, her coworkers, and her neighbors. She'd already written one of the generic tree cards to Evan, signing "fondly, Ruth" as she did for the others. The other neighbors' cards were already in their mailboxes.

Tomorrow, she'd take some time to read through the special cards in the pharmacy, even though she doubted she'd find something appropriate—something that implied a relationship just a small step above friendship. Still, what if Evan gave her a card that expressed more than she was willing to express? With six days left before the 25th, Ruth knew she'd be thinking about that until she finally made a decision.

Chapter 19

Ruth settled on a gift tag. As she suspected, none of the cards in the pharmacy were appropriate. The "friend" cards weren't enough, and the "someone special in my life" cards were too much. She vetoed the first three because the word *love* was included in the sentiment. Others were eliminated by phrases like *until you came into my life* and *you'll forever have my heart.* The cutout snowman gift tag was cute and practical and safe.

At the last minute, Ruth decided she needed something new to wear. Two days before Christmas (the eve of the eve), she entered the lone department store in the downtown area on her lunch hour. She rarely shopped there, and when she did, there were generally only a couple of other shoppers. Not today. She hadn't considered how many people waited until the last minute to prepare for the holidays, including a number of older men who looked desperate. She overheard one talking with the salesclerk.

"My wife's size? Oh, about your size. Maybe taller?"

The sales woman tried another question, but his puzzled look remained.

"Her favorite color? I have no idea. Well, her car is blue, kind of a light blue. Although she picked out green paint for the bedroom."

There were more racks than usual, a tight maze that didn't allow much space to pass between. Twinkle lights circled the ceiling and Christmas music played loudly. Ruth didn't know where to start.

A saleswoman saw the crestfallen, confused look on the novice shopper's face, and offered to help.

"I'm Sally, and I bet you're looking for something to wear for the holidays." When Ruth nodded, she pressed forward with questions.

"Dress, pants, skirt?" Dress.

"Size?" Eight.

"Did you have a color or style in mind?" Simple. Black or a dark color.

Within minutes, the saleswoman had ushered Ruth back to a dressing room, placing the hangers on two hooks.

"Try this group on first. I think you'll like them, and I can find other sizes if needed," she said, pointing to the right hook. "Then give these a try—try to keep an open mind," she added, gestured to the left. "They may not look like something you'd usually wear, but the holidays are for trying new things!"

Are they? Is that what the holidays are really about? Ruth wondered as the woman left and closed the curtain.

The dresses on each side were noticeably different. On the right— simple washable fabrics, ungarnished, clean lines. On the left—dry clean only for sure, sparkles, touches of ribbons and tiny beading.

She dutifully followed the directions, with saleswoman Sally popping back to check fit. Ruth was surprised by her honesty.

"This one doesn't do anything for you."

"Too plain—move to the next one."

"Let's return that one immediately to the shelf—it makes you look frumpy."

Truth told, Ruth had always thought of herself as somewhat frumpy. She brightened a bit when she considered, *maybe it's not me, I'm picking the wrong clothes!*

In the end, she faced a decision—one from each hook. The one on the right was simple, practical. She could wear it again to work with a cardigan sweater, and out in the evening for dinner with Evan. But there was something magical about the other dress. Perfectly holiday appropriate. Pretty beading at the top, a beautiful shade of green that was only around at Christmas. Sally patiently awaited her decision.

"I'll take this one," she said, holding up the Christmas dress.

"I was hoping you would," Sally said. "You could always buy the other one, too—I know it was a hard decision."

Ruth looked at the price tags again. "Unfortunately, over my budget."

Sally smiled. "You do know everything in the store is 50% off this week?"

She bought them both. Sally agreed to hold the dresses behind the counter so Ruth didn't have to hang them in the back room of the pharmacy. She picked them up after work.

The weather was even colder today, but Ruth didn't mind the walk home. She envisioned herself in the Christmas green dress, meeting Evan's aunt and uncle. Exchanging presents by the tree. She thought of herself in the black dress, meeting Evan after the holidays at the restaurant, seeing him seated at the table when she arrived, his face brightening.

She stopped to collect her mail just as Granston pulled up and rolled down his window.

"Everything going well Ruth?"

"Yes—everything is fine!"

"You'll be in staying here this week?"

"I'll be around—just local visits."

"Kevin mentioned he'd be out of town this week, and Lou said they'd be away during Christmas. Keep an eye out and call me if you see anything unusual."

"Thanks—I will."

As he drove away, Ruth wondered how anything could be more unusual than living with the dead in a graveyard.

Chapter 20

Loretta was up early the morning of Christmas Eve. She'd already showered, dried her hair, and added some cursory makeup to her face. Lou was still asleep. She decided to give him a little longer, hoping the smell of brewing coffee would wake him. It did.

"Merry Christmas, Letta, he said, yawning. "Why'd you let me sleep?"

"Figure you needed it. Build up some extra energy before seeing the grandkids," she smiled.

Grandkids. Whenever she said the word, her mind shifted to Michael. Surely the grandkid who needed them the most. Needed someone or something for sure. For at least five years, he'd been at the top of her prayer list.

Lou shuffled into the bathroom, his slippers scuffing on the floor. *When did he start shuffling?* Loretta noticed he'd been moving slower these days. *Another reason to live here—someplace manageable, maintenance-free.*

She could hear the shower starting up in the bathroom. Loretta allowed herself a minute to sip her coffee at the small table for two and look around. No tree with its ceramic-faced angel at the top, passed down from her parents. No ornaments—heirlooms, gifts, handmade by the kids and grandkids. Still, it looked festive. There was a large, fresh pine wreath on the exterior and interior of the door. Pine garland strung across the wall in the sitting area. Her antique creche on the coffee table. Lou had glued the shepherd's arm on again this year. She'd be sure to wrap the shepherd in bubble wrap for storage.

***

Lunch preparations were easy. She pulled out her clam chowder from the fridge and added it to her crock pot. She'd warm her homemade bread in the oven later. Her daughter was bringing a large salad to pair with Loretta's "famous" Thousand Island dressing. Simple meal. They'd have a larger meal tonight at the resort.

Borrowed folding chairs were already set up outside, and she had a stack of blankets ready. Everyone couldn't fit inside comfortably at the same time, but she liked the idea of hosting her family here for lunch on Christmas Eve. It would feel more like home once they were all here. *Would they all be here?*

A couple of weeks ago, her son Charlie told Loretta that Michael would be there. That he was working the program seriously and was finally on the road to recovery. But a week later, Charlie didn't mention Michael at all. And Loretta didn't ask.

Once again, her mind turned to Michael. When he was with the family, there was an unease. A feeling that matched an expression she remembered from her childhood—waiting for the other shoe to drop. But when he wasn't with the family, there was an unspoken emptiness. A missing piece. Her daughter told Loretta she was the heart of the family. If she was the heart, what part did the rest of the family play? Lou was the soul, the moral compass. The one who always did the right thing, even when it was hard. Painful. Like downsizing to a more manageable space.

Her daughter Leslie was the brain. Smart from the first day of the first year of school. Charlie was the arms, always doing. A helper. And her eldest Robert was the legs—couldn't sit still. An avid runner and tennis player.

What part was Michael? She slowly refilled her coffee, thinking about her grandson. Her grandson *before*. Before the drugs. Before the lying. Before the stealing. Before the long, emotional phone calls with her son and daughter-in-law. Before the disappearances. First for a night. Then weeks, months. Before his parents' frantic drives around their city, looking for him in the worst of places. Hoping not to find him there, and then hoping they would find him there, anywhere. Loretta pacing. Lou sitting in silence. Both willing the phone to ring, to hear he was safe. To hear he was back with family. And to hear he was the tender-hearted, clever, thoughtful grandson they had once known.

Before he was the other Michael. The one who didn't care about himself. Didn't comb his hair, wash his clothes, take a shower. The one who lied. The one who stole.

But not everything changed. The same insightfulness, there from an early age, remained. Watching, observing. A carefulness, a desire to know more--gifting him to see things that others didn't, even see things that were still to be. Michael was the eyes.

Chapter 21

Loretta and Lou's new home survived the family luncheon. The matriarch ran a tight ship for family functions, even more necessary in the tight quarters. Since only a limited number fit inside the home, all the grandchildren, plus her eldest son Robert sat outside, and a makeshift game of tag erupted.

"Don't step on people," Robert called out as the kids ventured toward the grave sites.

Loretta shook off a chill when she heard him. One of the "people" was Robert's first child. And Loretta's precious granddaughter. She'd lived only two weeks, but her grandmother held her tiny fist inside the incubator, making a silent vow to forever hold a place in her heart for Sonia.

She wasn't the only grandchild missing that day. As Charlie arrived, he looked straight at her and shook his head slightly. When she hugged him, he whispered, "He's still in the rehab—where he needs to be." She willed herself not to cry, and hugged him tighter. *It's where he needs to be.*

Later, as they pulled into the resort, Loretta took a deep breath, determined that she would focus on everyone who was *here*. She felt lucky that she and Lou had each other, and so many people who loved them. Pulling up her scarf up to protect her neck from the icy wind as they walked into the resort, her daughter Leslie looped her arm through Loretta's, then stopped suddenly.

"Look, mom! It's like we've stepped into one of those overly predictable Christmas movies!"

Long-needled pine trees edged the walkway, decorated with sparkling gold and red stars. The strands of light were dim in the early evening light, but night would reflect the full effect. The tiny white lights also wove through the thick garland over the entrance doors, flanked by two tall pines, stretching up to the top of the portico.

Loretta smiled. "I guess this beats the plastic garland we strung around the old house when you kids were little."

"Or the popcorn strands we made for the tree?" Leslie asked.

"Well, those decorations had a certain charm," Loretta said. "But I'm ready for something new. Something over the top for just this once."

"Change is good," Leslie said. And they walked together to start a different, but lovely Christmas.

Chapter 22

Kevin's morning Uber ride from the airport to his childhood home reminded him--Philly knew how to do the holidays. Evergreen wreathed doors, light-strung Christmas trees, along with store front windows edged in faux snow, complimented by the real stuff. Snow was lightly coating the sidewalks and roads. And still falling. He felt a swelling in his chest. It was hard not to miss Northwestern Philly this time of the year.

His father sounded brighter on the phone, his voice quickening when they talked about the Eagles' season. "We could go all the way again," his dad would repeat. "Two consecutive Super Bowl wins. Wouldn't that be somethin'?"

Kevin smiled. He was nowhere near the sports enthusiast that his father was, but that kind of passion could be contagious. And, not surprisingly, his father was wearing his Eagles Wentz jersey when he opened the door.

"My boy, my boy! Come in here!"

His father gave him the kind of full hug he remembered from the time when his mother was still alive. Maybe the light, the energy was back.

Kevin pulled back. "You're looking good, dad. Really good."

"OK, well there's a bit more of me these days," he said patting his stomach. "I'm gonna outgrow my jersey if your auntie doesn't stop sending me so many baked goods."

"I hope you saved some for me," Kevin laughed.

"I had to put a couple tins away in the cupboard so I didn't go through them all," he smiled.

Kevin didn't really care about the treats, although his auntie was known for her baking skills. He was fixed on seeing Kia. And his father knew him well.

"Why don't you put your luggage in your room—do you need a little nap before we leave?" he asked. "Get any sleep on the plane?"

"I'm pretty good on the red-eye, especially because I had a window seat. No nap needed. Let me just splash a little water on my face."

"Let me know if you need anything. I'll be ready when you are."

Kevin's bedroom still looked the same. Maybe his father pretended he still lived there so he didn't feel so alone. The Eagles and Phillies' memorabilia his dad bought him on game days. A wave of green, along with red, white, and blue. Pendants, a couple of signed baseballs on stands, bobbleheads, several caps on hooks, a giant Eagles' bedspread. The built-in shelves held old textbooks, trophies from his little league years, pictures of the twins together. Kevin in his little league uniform, posing next to Kia. At his school concert, trumpet in hand, posing next to Kia. At his high school, and then his college graduations, always posing next to Kia.

His life had a timeline. He looked closer. His face seemed to reflect a growing maturity, confidence. Kia had the same tight smile in each picture. Her hairstyle and clothes changed, but she did not.

The thought crept back into his mind again, the unthinkable that tried to push its way in now and then. *Would it have been better if she'd never been born?*

Just like always, he thought of his mother's words: *she's perfect.* And she was. Kevin couldn't imagine any other person who could give him as much joy as Kia did. She was unlike anyone he had ever known, and not because of her severe limitations. She expected so little. He knew it was slightly off, but every time he dated someone new, he compared them to Kia. The date who was rude to the waiter. Gossiped about coworkers. Couldn't bother to help their parents. Spoiled, entitled. Did life do that to them, or did they start out that way? Of course, others may think of Kevin in the same way, leaving for school and moving across the country when his family needed him.

His father's voice startled him.

"Lots of memories on that shelf," he said from the door.

"I think my hair's changed the most," he laughed. "Maybe I'm just kidding myself. Shouldn't wrinkles around the eyes wait until at least 30?"

"Oh, really? You're gonna talk about wrinkles to me?"

"You look good, dad. Better since before…the best I've seen you in a long time. More settled."

"I'm feeling good these days. Still got some livin' left."

"You need to come out to the other coast for a visit. That's assuming you don't get claustrophobic in small spaces!"

They laughed. Kevin had sent his father a description and pictures of his new home.

"As long as you like it," he said. "I'll like it, too. Besides, takes me longer to get around these days, so the smaller the better!"

"You'll love the waterfront. There's a great little diner within walking distance. They even have apple cobbler."

"As good as your mother's?" he asked, his voice cracking slightly.

"Not made with that much love—but a solid second place," he said. "You just let me know when you're ready. I'll make the arrangements, take off while you're there."

"I've been thinkin' about it. Would be good to visit cousin Milt while I'm there. You know his cancer's back?"

Kevin shook his head. He'd need to get over to visit him early in the new year.

"He's in good spirits," his dad continued. "Did he tell you, you got family in your neighborhood?

"What? In Heritage—the town?"

"No, no. Right in your…what do you call it anyway? A community? A grave yard?"

"In Coastal View?"

His father nodded. "That's right. Your cousin Melvin."

"I wonder why Uncle Milton never mentioned?" Kevin asked. His cousin passed while he was in college, and the family didn't make the trip out to the west coast. "I had no idea."

"Maybe Milt didn't want to spook you."

"Oh, like the ghost of Melvin's coming to haunt me?"

His dad laughed. "Well you know if anybody's doing some hauntin' it would be Melvin!"

"You're not wrong about that," Kevin said, thinking about his cousin's fun-loving personality. "When you come out, we'll visit Melvin and Milt."

"How about this summer? Just thinking we could spend some time outside in the warmer weather."

"Summer would be great—good time of year. We can do some fishing."

"You sure it's not too soon? Don't want you to lose your job. I feel like you just started. Do you even have leave to take off a few days?"

He felt his shoulders lighten as he turned to look directly at his father. "It's not too soon, dad."

"I can't wait to tell my poker buddies I'll be staying in a graveyard!"

Chapter 23

Champ walked through the entrance garden, with seasonal color from ornamental cabbage, red holly berries, and evergreens. He walked up the wide brick staircase to the carved front doors, placing his hand briefly on the knob, then moving it to the doorbell. He heard the familiar chime within the house and waited for his father to open the door. Social protocols were always a mystery to Champ, complicated by the fact that he lived here once. Should he wait for his father to open the door? The key to the house was still in his pocket, but maybe the locks were changed. Better to not know.

"Well, you're early, I think. A bit early," the elder Theodore said as he opened the door.

Champ swallowed but said nothing. Another mistaken protocol. He'd arrived a half-hour before the appointed dinner time.

It was understood that Champ would spend Christmas with his father. Easter, Father's Day, Thanksgiving, and Christmas. And both of their birthdays. Theodore Russell IV had visited his son's house exactly once. On the day he visited Piper's grave for her birthday. To prevent a future surprise, Champ took note that his father might "pop by" each year on that day.

Once Piper was gone, it took Theodore exactly three days to realize he couldn't bear living alone with his son.

Champ heard noises in the kitchen and knew that would be Kristina, the longtime family housekeeper and cook. She nodded at Champ without smiling.

"You're early."

"I said so," echoed Theodore.

Champ moved toward the dining room, the table fully dressed with the same beige linens that made an appearance on Thanksgiving. His mother was more creative with linens, red tablecloth and green napkins for Christmas. Her other touches were missing as well. No fresh pine centerpiece. No garland wrapped around the chandelier. No candles. No third place setting. His mother's chair was pushed in flush with the table, as if to prevent anyone from forgetting and settling in her space. There was no evidence of Christmas anywhere as far as Champ could tell.

What did he miss most? So many things. The smell of his mother's apple spice cake, cooling from the oven. The giant, long-needled Christmas tree with ornaments collected on family travels. The carefully-wrapped gifts with gold bows. He finally decided what he missed the most. The red velvet Christmas stockings hanging on the mantle, a polar bear, penguin, and reindeer (in that order), with carefully stitched names across the tops: Dad, Mom, Champ.

Dinner was at least familiar. There was the beef wellington Kristina always prepared on this day, along with popover rolls, green beans, and mashed potatoes. As the last serving dish was on the table, she put on her coat. "I'll return later to clean up."

The meal proceeded without comment, for which Champ was grateful. After they finished, his father returned with an envelope. "This seemed the most useful," he said, handing it to Champ.

"Should I open it now?" Champ asked.

"That's customary."

But it wasn't customary. Gifts were always exchanged in front of the tree, the heat from the fireplace encircling them.

Champ opened the envelope and slid out the contents.

"Buy yourself something you need," his father said.

There were five hundred-dollar bills inside. He thumbed through them with effort. All stiff and new.

Champ retrieved his jacket and pulled out a small box, which the shop owner had thoughtfully wrapped after asking if the purchase was a gift. The shiny red bow on the top had flattened. Every year, Champ had bought his parents a small crystal animal. His mother always made such a fuss and insisted on placing each one on the "animal shelf" in the dining room. This year, he'd selected an elephant. His father didn't talk about animals as much as his mother, but his father's desk had a wooden elephant bookend. Champ looked over his father's shoulder at the shelf, and his heart beat a little faster as he envisioned his father placing the elephant there with the other figurines.

"I'll open this later," Theodore Senior said, sliding it over next to his fork, crusted with the remains of the meal.

He wanted to tell his father it was customary to open the box. To be careful—it was delicate. He wanted to tell him he'd selected the elephant just for him. To tell him he understood that he missed her, because Champ missed her too. Instead he just sat quietly, a mirror image of his father.

He wondered if there was dessert. But his father left the table and settled into his reading chair, picking up the newspaper.

Champ folded his envelope with the hundred-dollar bills and slid it into his pants pockets. He pulled on his coat from the rack by the door. His father looked back and raised his hand in farewell.

He left without his mother's customary good-bye hug. Her whispered "go with God" after she kissed him on the cheek every day when he left for school and later for work. In the foyer, Champ tried to feel his mother's warmth against him—love transferred to him —her only child. When he'd wondered why he didn't have a sibling, his mother told him, "I only need my dear Champ."

Outside, the air was colder than he thought. He pulled out his thick mittens from his pockets, put them on, and started walking. He remembered he'd forgotten to wish his father a Merry Christmas and wondered for a moment if he should return. Then he realized his father hadn't wished him one either.

Chapter 24

Ruth balanced herself on the sidewalk, a shopping bag in each hand. The gifts were heavier than expected. She hadn't considered it when purchasing the books, but she was thankful she didn't select especially large volumes. A good upper body workout for sure. The slightly slower walk to her aunt's house gave her more time to think.

She'd briefly thought about inviting Evan to Midnight Mass, and today to lunch, but ultimately decided against both. She wasn't ready for those formal introductions. Besides, she insisted (many times) she wanted to "take things slow." Recently, Evan added "for now" after her phrase, which always made Ruth smile.

As much as she tried to push it away, revealing the secret would likely cause the relationship to crumble. And the longer she held on to the secret, the less likely he'd forgive her.

How would that look? The two in such proximity every day. Would he wave if he saw her returning from the mailbox? Would she wave at him? Would she continue to dine alone at the places they frequented?

Ruth physically shook her head, then put her bags down for a moment, rotating her shoulders to alleviate all the weight she felt. Not just from the books. Then she reminded herself, *Today is Christmas.* And, with a deep breath and a forced smile, she picked up her bags and continued the remaining four blocks.

Sounds from inside the house radiated through the door as she reached the first step. Ruth smiled. Her cousins' children were always so excited on Christmas. Other days as well, but especially on Christmas.

As she opened the door, the littlest ran into Ruth from the side, one of the shopping bags landing on the floor with a thump.

"Ooops! Merry Christmas," Addie laughed, showing her missing front tooth.

"Let's let cousin Ruth get her coat off, shall we," her aunt called out, peering around the doorway from the kitchen.

"Not to worry," she said, laughing as the little one started pulling out boxes from the dropped bag. "Santa's helper will place these under the tree for me."

Addie gleefully complied and Ruth added gifts from the second bag to the pile before moving to the kitchen and placing a tin printed with ivy leaves on the small dessert table.

"What have you there?" her aunt asked.

"Gingerbread cookies," she said, lifting the lid and tilting toward her so she could have a view.

"They look too perfect to be homemade. Grauler's bakery?"

"Truly, I made them! Although technically I helped make them. Evan did most of the work. I just followed his directions. His mother's recipe."

"Evan—how impressive! A young man who can bake. That's a rarity."

"Oh mom, I don't think it's that much of a rarity," her cousin's husband said. "Lots of men know how to bake."

"Oh Thomas? Do you bake?"

His face reddened. "No mom, I don't bake. But others do…"

"Well, I suppose Ruth's Evan isn't the only one," she said, turning to face Ruth. "Did you decide to invite him to join us?"

"I just thought it might be a bit early for a family gathering."

"You won't see him at all today?" her aunt said, as though she already knew the answer.

"Later, for dinner."

"Just the two of you?"

"Actually, no. His aunt and uncle. They live just a couple of houses down from the marina," she said, trying to shift the conversation a bit. "Just across from the old parsonage."

Her aunt smiled, "Next time, Ruth. We'd love to meet him."

"Of course. Thank you—I know he'd love to meet all of you, too."

"Well, you certainly look beautiful today. I should have known you wouldn't get this fancied up for just us," she said, smiling.

"Hot chocolate?" Thomas asked. "Extra whipped cream as usual?"

Ruth nodded, her face starting to warm after her aunt's compliment.

"See mom, I made hot chocolate!"

"Well, you were certainly proficient at stirring it as it warmed--after I added all the ingredients."

"And, he did remember that I like extra whipped cream, that should count, too—shouldn't it?" Ruth asked.

"Doesn't everyone here like extra whipped cream?" her aunt countered. "Except for Lenora who is lactose intolerant."

"Glad you reminded me," Thomas said, as he ladled out another mug.

Ruth was just glad the topic had changed. It seemed Evan wasn't the only one hoping the relationship would grow more serious.

The bag (just one this time) felt light when she stepped out on the porch, the background noise quieting once the oversized front door closed, sounds further reduced with each step until she no longer heard the excitement from inside her aunt's house.

Evan, she thought. *Spending the rest of Christmas with Evan.* She focused on that thought to push out the reality that she'd meet his relatives for the first time. Thankfully, just two of them. She knew Evan must be sad he wasn't spending Christmas with his mother and siblings—his first one without them.

Faulty weather forecasts—this one was a major miss. No blizzard. No snow accumulation. No ice. Today was cold, but clear and bright. He might be sad, but the poor prediction was good fortune for her.

The sun had already set, the almost full moon especially bright without clouds. She realized her pace was quicker now. Whether due to the lighter load, or something else, she was nearly there. She'd been fairly certain about the specific house, but took a preview walk a few days ago just to be absolutely sure.

"I'm so glad you're here," Evan said, opening the door. "Let me take this—"

"My presents from my aunt's house," she said, handing over the bag and taking over her coat. "Oh—your gingerbread cookies were consumed immediately! Everyone loved them. My aunt is impressed that you bake."

"A group effort," he said, smiling back as he took her coat. "Your dress—it's beautiful. Ruth, look beautiful—"

She smiled, then realized she'd left something in the bag. "Oh, there's a tin of vanilla fudge for your aunt and uncle in there."

He pulled it from the bag. "That's thoughtful—from Gauler's?"

She shook her head. "Why does everyone keep saying that? I made the fudge. Really. I know I don't often cook or bake."

"You're full of secrets, aren't you?"

Her heart pounded faster, and then a couple came around the corner. She could immediately see a resemblance to his uncle— wavy light brown hair, shy crooked smile, slightly tall.

"Ruth—Aunt Ellen and Uncle Benny," he said, motioning.

"I must give you a hug," Ellen said, embracing her before there was a chance to respond. "It's just lovely to finally meet you, Ruth. You're as pretty as Evan described."

"Thank you, he's only said wonderful things about you both," she said, handing her the tin. "I've been looking forward to meeting you."

"Not as much as we have," Benny said. "We were starting to think Evan had an imaginary girlfriend!"

"Well, we are certainly happy you could join us tonight for dinner," Ellen said. "How was your time with your family today?"

She always felt the same crick in her neck, an involuntary bristle when anyone referred to her family. Even after all these years, Ruth didn't think of her aunt's family that way. Her family was with her in Coastal View.

As usual, Ruth answered gracefully. A brief description of the little ones' excitement, opening gifts around the tree.

"Sounds like an ideal Christmas Day," Ellen said.

"It was," she responded politely, stepping closer to the large pine tree in the great room. The tree nearly reached the top of the vaulted ceiling. The house had clearly been completely renovated at some point, although the exterior was misleadingly historic. "That's quite a tree," she said, looking at the glass ornaments—up and down, side to side. Each one leading to the next. "Stunning! Those ornaments! So beautiful, and so many!"

"It's my passion," Ellen said.

"Addiction," Benny countered.

"I actually grew tired of trimming the tree this year," Ellen said. "We might have to look for a smaller tree next Christmas."

"I've heard this three years in a row now," he laughed.

"I really mean it this year. I actually have the last box of ornaments in the closet—couldn't make the effort to add anymore."

Ruth wondered where the other balls could actually be placed—each branch had two or three ornaments. She had a flicker of a memory from childhood. She was helping her sisters wrap their handmade construction paper chain around a small pine tree cut from their yard—a pattern of red and green. The trees couldn't look more different, with her family's tree missing branches and dropping needles all over the floor. Ornaments made by children's unsophisticated hands using paper and pinecones. Although that same woodsy smell was precisely the same.

"Evan, you should really take that extra box home with you, use it to trim your tree. I could give you more next year."

"Aunt Ellen—you've seen my house! Maybe I have room for a table-top tree. A *small* table-top tree."

"You'll still be needing some ornaments."

"Put me down for a dozen—but only if they're miniatures," he laughed.

Ruth liked the easy banter between Evan and his family. He'd told her that they were important people in his life, and it was easy to see that. It was a feeling she'd craved for a long time.

Evan carried her shopping bag on the walk back to Coastal View. Christmas was always magical. Tonight, the stars were in full, brilliant view.

"I really like your aunt and uncle," she said softly, as Evan reached over and took her hand.

"They like you, too."

"You're just being nice. How could you possibly know that? Mind reading abilities you've been hiding from me?"

"Maybe because when you left to use the bathroom, they both told me," he laughed. "My uncle actually used the word 'terrific.' I don't think I've ever heard him describe anyone as terrific."

"Not even you?"

"Well, that goes without saying. I'm sure he thinks I'm *terrific*, but he's of that mindset that men don't share their feelings."

"I'm glad you're not like that," she said squeezing his hand.

"I could never manage to keep my feelings about you to myself, Ruth. I hope you know how much you mean to me."

Ruth looked up at the stars, wondering how she could possible deserve such a night as this. Maybe her mother was looking down, willing this entire day for her. Maybe this was her mother's way of sending a message that the family forgave her.

The couple had agreed to exchange gifts at Ruth's. She'd set up a small nativity scene on her end table, a cast-off from her aunt. And she'd clipped evergreens and fashioned into decorative sprigs with ribbon to tuck in here and there. She lit a pine candle to add to the scent. No tree, but she'd never match the tree at Evan's aunt and uncle's.

"Wine? Beer? Eggnog?"

"Did you actually make eggnog?"

"The fudge really was homemade, but the eggnog I bought," she laughed.

"Definitely—would love to try the eggnog."

Ruth poured two cups, then settled on the sofa next to Evan.

"A toast?" he asked, holding up his cup. She nodded and he thought for a moment.

"To the first of many Christmases together. Cheers." They clicked their glasses together and took a sip.

Evan certainly didn't keep his feelings to himself. Even when he was subtle the message came through.

"Present time?" she asked. "You open first."

She pulled a medium-sized gift bag toward him. No card, but she'd at least signed the gift card *Love, Ruth.*

He pulled out the first gift inside and unwrapped it slowly, like he was trying to preserve the paper.

"Oh, you're one of *tho*se kind of people," she teased.

"My mother taught us to not waste," he said, with mock seriousness, finally unveiling the present. "Craig Johnson! You remembered how much I liked Longmire!"

"I hope you enjoy the books as much as the show."

Ruth had purchased the first four books in a series of 16. She'd actually added sticky notes to the front of each with the number—so he could read in order.

Evan looked at each cover, reading the title aloud. "The Cold Dish…Death Without Company…Kindness Goes Unpunished… Another Man's Moccasins." He leaned over and kissed her. "You are so thoughtful."

"There's more in there, and more paper to save," she smiled.

He continued his careful unwrapping with the last two gifts—a coffee press and a bag of *Cool Breeze.*

"I've been told the press will help you with your quest to make your own iced coffee. And the coffee was ground specifically for the press."

Evan was already reading the directions on the back of the press. The coffee was sealed, but the scent leaked through into the air.

"OK, the eggnog is great, but I'm suddenly craving a cup of coffee," he said. "I take back my statement that you are thoughtful. You are *incredibly* thoughtful. Seriously."

He gave Ruth a hug and a quick kiss on the cheek before returning his gifts to the bag and folding the paper.

"OK, your turn now. I suddenly wish I'd bought more," he said, handing her a box wrapped in green metallic paper and topped with a red velvet bow.

The box was the size that would hold a large coffee mug. She placed it on her lap and removed the bow first.

"Please don't take it personally that I'm not a professional unwrapper like you! I'm always too excited to take my time." And just as she said it, she quickly tore the paper from the box, lifting the lid. Inside was another box, this one much smaller and unwrapped. A blue velvet box that Ruth instinctively knew contained jewelry. In a single moment, she pulled out the box and opened, seeing Evan from the side staring at her.

A silver necklace. Two dainty linked hearts. She'd never owned a piece of fine jewelry, or anything so beautiful.

"I'm not one to cry," she said, her voice cracking slightly. "But this will test me."

"I know your cross necklace is special to you, but I thought maybe you could wear this at the same time—the chain is shorter."

She was surprised when Evan mentioned the cross. She'd never said anything about it. It was rather large and the chain long, so she usually wore it beneath her clothes. But it was a gift from someone special. Just like this new necklace.

"Yes—the chain's much shorter," she said. "So delicate."

"Do you like it?"

Ruth nodded, carefully removing the necklace from the backing and letting the chain unroll. "Help me put it on," she asked, handing it to Evan, then turning and lifting her hair from her neck.

"Let's see—let me just—there. All hooked."

Ruth turned for him to see it, then got up to look in the mirror by the door. The light caught it as she moved. "I love it. Truly."

"I'm relieved," he said. "I've never bought a piece of jewelry before."

I'm glad I was the first, Ruth thought, surprising herself.

And as they sat there together, drinking a second glass of eggnog and talking about the day, Ruth realized something she'd been fighting. She wanted this. She wanted to spend every Christmas with Evan. She wanted something she'd lost a long time ago—a family of her own. And she wanted that with Evan. Tomorrow she'd take the first step by scheduling an appointment with someone she trusted. Father Anthony.

Chapter 25

The secrets you tell yourself, Loretta thought. Maybe one of the children grabbed the remaining coconut cookies from the jar as they were leaving on Christmas Eve, spreading crumbs on the counter. Maybe Lou had forgotten to check the lock on the back door. They never used it, but one of their children or grandchildren may have gone out that way. Definitely logical.

Maybe she'd misplaced the bank envelope that held $100. Loretta usually left the money on the dresser in the bedroom, but it wasn't there. She could have easily moved it when she was tidying up for the luncheon. Or Lou could have moved it. She could find out for sure by asking him, but she wouldn't. She could also do a more thorough search, but she wouldn't do that either. She'd rather not know.

But one thing she did know for sure—she'd made the coconut cookies for one person in particular. They were Michael's favorite.

Chapter 26

Two days after Christmas and the memories were still fresh. The weather was damp and bitterly cold, but she had more on her mind than the current temperature. All those Sundays after church, stopping at the flower shop then continuing to Coastal View to visit her family. Ruth walked the familiar route between Coastal View and St. Lawrence, but this time the walk was reversed. She had an appointment with Father Anthony.

She'd felt a connection to the priest. He'd only been at the parish for the last three or four years, so he wasn't there when her family died, although he surely knew the story. Especially with all the recent Coastal View publicity.

Still, when she talked to him briefly after Mass, she never saw the kind of pity most others showed. She still saw that pity in her aunt's eyes, her cousins'. She saw it on the faces of her boss and coworkers. Heard it in their voices. Even her three closest friends. One of them, Marjorie, had been with her that night. The other two were friends from high school. They'd all meet for dinner, and one of them would mention their mother, their father, a sibling, and then it would come. The awkward silence. Looking down at the table. Hastily changing the subject.

She was drawn to people who didn't seem to pity her. People she'd met more recently like a new coworker, her neighbors at Coastal View. Evan.

Just thinking of him made her smile, and her hand went instinctively to her necklace, rubbing it between her gloved finger and thumb. Making sure it was still there.

She only waited a couple of minutes before an elderly man left Father Anthony's office. Then he peaked around the corner with a big smile, his thick, curly black hair in more disarray than on Sunday mornings. "Ruth—please come in!"

The office was larger than she expected, with two loveseats facing each other, coffee table between, and a desk in the corner. "Coffee?" he asked. She shook her head and they took a seat across from one another. "Something special bring you here today, or just a friendly visit?"

"Something special," she said, thinking special probably wasn't the right word. "I'm looking for some advice. Long overdue. Way long overdue."

"Maybe you're looking for advice at just the right time," he said gently. "We all have our own timetable."

"That's a nice way to think about it, Father. I just—well, hard to know how to start," she said, feeling heat rising up her neck.

"I have all the time you need, Ruth. Really. No other appointments. Take your time. We can even talk about something else if you like. How was your Christmas?"

She smiled, and again found herself rubbing her necklace. "I had a lovely Christmas. I hope you had the same?"

"I did. Of course there's the added pressure of all those Easter-Christmas Catholics in the church. Thinking that if I get the homily just right—the words and my delivery—maybe they'll be back next week."

"I never thought of it like that," Ruth said. "I'm sure it's not a reflection of you, Father Anthony!"

"Still, I suppose that's the optimist in me, hoping the church will be filled next week," he laughed.

"Maybe your optimism will rub off on me today," she said slowly. "I'm looking for your optimism and your wisdom I suppose. It's related to a secret in my life."

"Well, we all have them, Ruth. You're not alone."

"But some secrets are worse than others, aren't they?" She didn't wait for an answer. "There's a secret, a serious one that I've held onto for a long time. Something I haven't been able to share, or forgive myself for."

"Have you prayed about it?"

"More times than I could ever remember. I do know that God has forgiven me. At least, I hope so."

"If you're sincerely sorry and you've asked, God has not only forgiven you, he's actually forgotten what you've done."

"It's a pretty big one to forget," she said.

"That's why God is God. Definitely easier for Him to forgive us than for us to forgive ourselves."

Ruth took a deep breath. "I'm sure you've heard what happened to my family."

Father Anthony nodded, and Ruth looked closely in his eyes. She saw compassion, but not pity.

She spoke quickly, before she could change her mind. "I caused the fire. It was me. I caused the deaths of my mother, father, sisters, and brother."

"I don't know the details, Ruth—that was before I arrived at St. Lawrence," he moved in closer. "Did you set the fire on purpose?"

It was a logical question, but it surprised her. "Well, no. I—no I didn't purposely set the fire."

"So it was accidental?"

"Yes—accidental, but still my fault."

"Did you want it to happen?"

"No—of course not. I loved my family," she said, picturing each in her mind. "I miss them. Every day."

"OK, if you're comfortable, let's walk through it. What happened that day?"

She took a deep breath.

"The day was…just a regular Saturday. Although I was excited because I'd been invited to a sleep-over party that night. I knew all the girls, but was only close to one of them. The other girls—they were more popular. I was surprised, excited to get the invitation." Another deep breath. "I remember wanting to make a good impression—so they'd like me. Wore my cutest dress. Packed my nicest sleepshirt. I just really, really wanted to fit in—thought I could be part of their group at school." Another breath. "And my hair. I wanted to make sure it looked nice. My mother had found a flat iron for me at the second-hand store. Still brand-new in the box. She knew how much I wanted one. I'd tried it out the weekend before when I had more time than on school mornings. I thought it made me look more grown up."

Father Anthony tilted his head and pursed his lips.

"Oh, I'm guessing you don't know what a flat iron is? It's an electric device—like a regular iron but for hair. You slide your hair between the two sections and it flattens it out—makes it sleek, shiny."

He just nodded, then waited for her to speak.

"I used it that day, before I left for the party. I used it and I remember leaving and feeling so proud of myself," her voice cracked. "Probably the last time I've felt that way—proud of myself. I wanted to look good for those girls. And my family died because of it."

Ruth sat back, her head down.

"Maybe I missed something, Ruth—you left for the party? You weren't there when the fire started?"

"I wasn't there, but the flat iron was. I left it plugged in. I remember when I arrived at her house, the girl who was hosting the party went on and on about how I should wear my hair like that all the time. And while she was talking, a little thought hit me—I left it plugged in. And then she pulled me into the other room where the other girls were. And another girl started talking about my hair, even feeling it and saying how she wanted her hair to look so smooth. And then I didn't think about it again. Never thought about it until that night when the phone call came."

Ruth put her shaking hands over her eyes for a moment. "That's what happened. That's how the fire started."

Father Anthony put his hand to his mouth. A moment of careful consideration before he spoke. "Who told you, Ruth? Who told you how the fire started? Was it a family member? Someone from the fire department?"

Ruth eyes grew narrow. She looked off to the side for a moment. "I know what you're asking. But no one told me. They didn't have to. I already knew."

"It's certainly possible, Ruth. Even if it were possible, don't electric devices have built in timers that turn off after they've been left unused for some time? I press enough white shirts to know that regular irons do."

"I, I'm not sure. I guess that one didn't," she said, supposing the one her mother bought must have been a cheaper model—the family budget didn't allow top-of-the-line products even if they were from the second-hand store.

"OK, let's just take a step back. I think the first thing you'll want to confirm is what actually caused the fire."

"But I—"

"You've only assumed what caused the fire. No actual proof. Right?"

She nodded.

"The Fire Chief would certainly have the cause. I know the old Chief retired just last year and moved away to Florida, but certainly

Chief Jackson would know, or at least have all the records."

Ruth felt unsteady. Just the thought there could be another cause overwhelmed her. And now there was the chance to know for sure.

"I could certainly give Chief Jackson a call, Ruth. You could call him yourself of course. If you'd like some company, I'd be glad to go with you."

"This is—a lot. You've given me a lot to consider. Can I let you know?"

"Of course, Ruth—remember what I said about that timeline. It's your timeline and your timeline only."

She stood up. "I have to get to work, Father. This has been good—useful. Truly. I just need to think about it a little more, OK?"

"Absolutely."

On her walk to work, she realized she could be a different person. The secret had covered her in shame. Unworthy of happiness. Unworthy of a real relationship with Evan.

Should she make the appointment with the Chief immediately? That way there would be no question. But first, there was another question to answer.

Did she want to know for sure? Would it be better just to allow herself to imagine that there was another cause? That she didn't cause her family and Evan's father to die?

Chapter 27

The scrutiny on Coastal View security wasn't going away. Despite Granston's connection to local and state law enforcement, despite his vigilance in ensuring all leads away from the community were passed forward--the attention remained. And now, federal law enforcement was involved. The F-B-I. The theory of sex trafficking had been introduced. In his first meeting with the lead agent, he tried to gather as much information as possible. As much as he hated to think about it, he'd need to update Bill Rafferty again. He'd asked for a status when something substantial or "something that could become substantial" occurred, and the FBI's involvement certainly fit the criteria. Along with the upcoming interviews.

The FBI requested interviews with all Coastal View residents and any employees on site during the timeframe when the missing young woman was spotted on the security camera. Fortunately, the numbers were still small. In a couple of months, new owners in Section Two would begin moving into the community. Section Three would overlap, starting another month later. There was constant construction, and Granston insisted the general contractor keep an accurate accounting of each individual onsite, with times in and out. It was important he show Bill Rafferty how seriously he took this position. Despite his part-time work with the Sheriff's Department, he kept a strategic view while continuing to work at a tactical level—keeping tabs on residents' comings and goings, patrolling the interior and even the exterior of the community by car and on foot.

Granston had the time. His last serious relationship ended a year ago. He knew other men appreciated women who were independent, but not him. At least, not to the extent that she'd exhibited. They'd been together for six months, yet Cheryl didn't tell Granston she was changing jobs. Or going on a weekend trip with her sister. When she mentioned that she was moving, he ended it. Definitely a pattern of behavior. Or maybe she just didn't like Granston.

Chapter 28

He'd carefully considered his arrival time. He always strove to arrive first, but not so early that the host felt uncomfortable. At precisely 11:55 a.m., Granston arrived to New Year's Brunch.

"Happy New Year," Lou shouted as he opened the door. Granston could see Loretta behind him.

"Happy New Year to you, as well," he responded.

"Please, come in, come in—get out of the cold."

He stepped in as Loretta was pulling a large casserole dish out of the oven—a combination of egg and seafood judging by the aroma.

"Welcome!" she said over her shoulder.

"Let me take your coat," Lou said. "And to drink—iced tea, mimosa, coffee?"

"Thank you, Lou. I'll take a coffee."

"Definitely a good choice for the weather. Although give those mimosas consideration—Loretta does something special to them."

He could see the pitcher on the countertop with stemmed glasses on the side.

"Maybe later."

"Have a seat and I'll get your that coffee—cream, sugar?"

"Just a little cream."

The door bell sounded. Kevin, and right behind him were Ruth and Evan.

Arriving together. Doesn't seem like they're trying to hide the relationship these days, Granston thought. He remembered the first time he saw them together in town, walking into the diner. It looked casual enough. They weren't holding hands. Evan held the door for her, which of course was the proper thing to do, but no sign that this was more than two neighbors having lunch. He took note each time he saw them. Small things. Evan leaning in when Ruth talked. His hand touching her shoulder. The two of them on Christmas night, going into Ruth's house after dark.

One by one, the guests talked about Christmas.

"How was your time in Philadelphia?" Lou asked Kevin.

"Wonderful. I forget how much I miss it there. My hometown really knows how to do Christmas! And, I think there's a few extra pounds to lose after my aunt's baking. She must have been at it for weeks."

Granston noticed his description seemed void of details about his family, except that his aunt liked to bake. Did he live with her before his arrival here?

"Sounds like you're close to her," Granston said. "I bet she misses you."

"That's what she tells me on every phone call," he laughed.

No additional detail. Granston couldn't ask too much or it would sound like what it was—an interrogation.

"How about you Evan—your aunt and uncle's place?" Kevin asked.

"Yes—starting with breakfast. What is it about aunts always wanting to feed you? I'm sure they had enough leftovers to feed everybody who works at the Marina."

"Another feeding frenzy at your family's?" Kevin asked, looking at Ruth.

"There was more than enough for sure. What I look forward to the most is hot chocolate—homemade. My cousin's husband always gets stuck with keeping it stirred on the stovetop," she laughed. "I try not to arrive too early so that duty doesn't get passed to me."

"Speaking of food," Loretta said from the kitchen (just a few steps away from the living area), brunch is served. Fruit salad, selection of cheeses, coconut and blueberry muffins, and my new recipe, Coastal View Casserole. Eggs, shrimp, crab, cheese. If anyone has an aversion to seafood, or cheese, I have some scrambled eggs here as well.

"Someone has to go first," Lou said rising.

"Lou—the guests go first!"

"OK—if you don't want me to be in trouble with my wife, will one of you step up?"

Ruth laughed. "Well, we can't have that, can we?" She moved in front of Lou and took a plate from the table. "Loretta, this all looks delicious!"

Evan predictably followed. "What a wonderful way to start the new year!"

Once they all filled their plates, conversation continued—mostly about the food itself. Granston noted there was no mention of Champ. Did he decline the invitation? Or was he wasn't invited?

The brunch ended with some general chatter about progress on Section Two. The models were slightly different in the new area.

"I probably shouldn't say this in front of law enforcement," Evan said, nodding at Granston, "But I had a look-see the other day in one of the models. I didn't care for the flow at all. When you're going tiny, it's definitely better to have an open feel."

"I've been wondering if any families are moving in," Loretta said. "I watch some of those TV shows about tiny houses, and saw one recently about a family of five and two dogs. Place was only slightly bigger than this. Had a first-floor bedroom like ours, but smaller. But had two sleeping lofts for the kids. I guess the dogs just have to fend for themselves!"

"Hopefully, they opted for the stairs to the loft," Ruth said. "I'd worry about kids climbing the ladders."

"There are some nights when I'm too almost too tired to climb that ladder myself," Kevin laughed.

"I've fallen asleep on the sofa a few times and just stayed there," Evan said. "Not enough energy to make the climb. My dad was a fireman—he'd be ashamed to hear me say that!"

Granston was in observation mode. Maybe he imagined it, but he was nearly certain Ruth's face grew pale with the mention of Evan's father.

Chapter 29

As the brunch was wrapping up, Granston said his goodbyes. He'd been the first to arrive, so it was logical to be the first to leave.

Loretta brought his coat. "Let me walk you out. I've gotten a bit overheated from standing near the oven this morning."

On the front porch, she dropped her voice. "I was wondering if you may have seen anyone around our house on Christmas Eve—after we all left."

"I didn't notice anything, at least at the time I was walking through."

She nodded.

"Was something wrong—a window open, a door ajar?"

Granston watched her carefully. She seemed uncertain about sharing more, maybe worried that would lead to more questions.

"The back door wasn't latched, but we had our family here before we left. Certainly could have been anyone of them."

He decided to take a light touch approach. Didn't want Loretta to feel uncomfortable. He wanted to build trusted relationships—not just for now, but also for the future.

"Did you notice anything different inside? Anything in a different place? Or something missing?"

Loretta paused. "Well, no. Nothing missing. I suppose someone just left the door open and we forgot to check."

"I'm sure that's the case. But intuition tends to be a good thing. I'll continue to keep an eye out, Loretta."

"Thanks, Granston—I'm sure it's nothing."

He nodded and walked back to his car as she headed back inside. He was certain Loretta was holding something back.

Chapter 30

Bill Rafferty's West Coast-East Coast red-eyes were becoming common place. He'd picked up some efficiencies from that first trip. He'd made the mistake of arriving at the departure gate three hours before take-off and then spent a full hour on the back end after the luggage carousel location changed three times, forcing him to stride from one end of baggage claim to another.

The driver dropped him at the airport entrance, and he proceeded directly to the Pre-Check security screening line. He held up his phone to show the attendant his boarding pass—he'd checked in at home—and proceeded toward the agent. There were only two people in front of him. On the other side of the screening, he grabbed his items from the plastic container and pulled his carryon off the belt. He wheeled it behind him as he headed toward the lounge. His frequent flyer status provided him with a few perks, including access to lounge amenities. At this point, he could certainly afford a lounge membership, but he followed his frugal uncle's advice—why pay for something when you can get it for free? He checked his watch. One hour before priority boarding.

At the sleek, chrome bar (*how did they manage to keep the fingerprints wiped away all day?*) he settled back with his gin and tonic and a small serving of cheese, nuts, and strawberries from the buffet. He didn't like to eat or drink heavily before the flight. A small snack combined with the same beverage seemed to do the trick. He'd sleep well and arrive rested for his interviews.

This trip, he had three appointments—an interview with a writer from *Forbes*, a meeting with potential investors, and a live interview on a popular, nationally-televised program. It was the last hour of the show, when most folks were headed to the office and only stay-at-homes were watching, but this was the first national broadcast publicity he'd garnered. Certainly more would follow.

He made a mental note to ask Granston about the current state of the investigation in the vicinity of Coastal View. He saw the FBI's involvement in this single incident as problematic at first, but Granston indicated that might speed the case along, eliminating all undue attention for good. Didn't want anything to unsettle potential investors.

That view seemed logical. Besides, Granston knew much more about security and law enforcement than he did—that's why he hired him. Still, he'd always found it a struggle to delegate to others, and even more of a struggle to trust people to do the job to his impeccable standards.

"Another?" the bartender asked, pointing to the nearly empty glass.

He waved him away, took out a tip and checked his watch again. Time to head to the gate.

Chapter 31

Kevin was considering adopting a cat. He'd had a dog for much of his childhood, but never a cat. Still the practical aspects of a cat were appealing. Even though he sometimes worked from home, his days in-office could be long, and he'd worry about letting the dog out. Even if he arrived home on time, he'd have to walk the dog over two blocks to the closest green area. Coastal View didn't have an area appropriate for a dog to relieve itself—there was even a clause in the settlement contract that spelled that out. Even without the clause, something about letting them go in a grave yard seemed incredibly disrespectful.

He felt even more connected to Coastal View after learning his cousin Melvin was buried here—Apostles Circle, third grave from the main drive. His death was a shock to all who knew him—the life of the party who was always teasing, joking. And the first to step up and help. It seemed unfair that something so mundane as an infection would remove him from the world.

Kevin wandered through the rows one day, reading the markers until he found it. He had so many memories of Melvin, many happy, but it was the one unhappy memory that sometimes crowded out the rest.

In Kevin's research of all things feline he realized that if he traveled for work, or even a visit back home, he'd need someone to come in and empty the litter box, fill the bowls with food and water. His mind immediately thought of Ruth. He'd seen her trying to (unsuccessfully) coax a feral cat closer.

Before he had a chance to ask her, he saw Champ at the mailbox. Kevin was immediately disappointed in himself. Why didn't he consider Champ first? He even worked at a veterinary office. Maybe this was a way to get to know him a little better. Kevin was a novice in the area of cats, but Champ was likely an expert.

Just because Champ had some challenges in socializing didn't mean people should give up on him. Maybe he took longer to feel comfortable around others, especially if people treated him differently because of how he looked—stumbling a bit when he walked, dropping his head, limiting his responses to a word or just a gesture. Kia had faced this all of her life. When he was young, Kevin didn't want to attend parties when Kia wasn't invited. That happened frequently, even the years when the two of them were in the same classroom—Kia with an aide by her side. Sometimes his parents gently suggested he go, especially when all boys from the same class where invited, or just a small group of core friends.

He decided to be prepared—have a list of questions in his head that he could ask Champ the next time he saw him. Maybe the one outsider in Coastal View would start to feel more like an insider.

Just two days later, he had his chance, feeling glad he'd spent some time thinking about the information he needed. Champ was headed to the mailbox just as Kevin walked out his door.

"Hey, Champ."

No response.

"I understand you know a lot about cats."

Champ kept walking, but he nodded.

"I'm thinking of adopting one."

Champ didn't look up, but stopped and turned his head in Kevin's direction.

"Could I ask you a few questions?"

His head rose. Kevin took that as a yes.

"Is there a shelter nearby that you'd recommend? A place that has cats for adoption?"

"Heaven's Door. Uh, you make a right out here," he said, pointing to the entrance. "Go six blocks, then make a left. Go another two blocks and it's there."

"Good place?"

"Yes. I volunteer there sometimes. Clean cages."

"Great—I will definitely check them out. Speaking of work, I know you work for the vet. What are their hours?"

"Monday, Tuesday, Wednesday, Thursday - 9 to 6. Saturday – 9 to 1. Closed Friday and Sunday."

Sounded well-rehearsed, Kevin thought. Probably had to memorize and recite to customers who asked. "What about emergencies— when the vets office is closed?"

"Special Care Pet Hospital," he answered quickly. "Always open. Twenty minutes away in Oceanside."

"This is really helpful, Champ—I'll write it all down when I get back inside."

"You can ask again if you forget."

"Thank you. I'll bring the cat in for a checkup, once I've found one that's a good fit. I guess a good fit for me and the cat."

"You'll need a list," Champ said. "A list of things the cat will need. I'll get you one from work tomorrow."

"That would be great, thanks again, Champ."

Maybe it was Kevin's optimism, but he thought he saw Champ smile when he turned to go.

The next day, Champ stood waiting at the mailbox, yellow paper in his hand. Kevin wondered how long he'd been standing there.

"Hey, Champ—good to see you again!"

"I have your list from the vet. You can get everything at the pet store on Main. My coworker said some things are cheaper online."

Kevin already knew he'd only order online if the item wasn't available in the local store—he was trying to support the small businesses, but even more, he was always looking for ways to build a sense of community through personal relationships. Of course he had his colleagues at work—most of them around his age. The usual gatherings were at a local brewery where they would talk about tech —an extension of the workday. But he'd also established a few casual friendships with folks in the area, through a dart league at the pub. Not something he ever thought he'd try, but he enjoyed it and his hand-eye coordination was decent. And, unlike his Silicon Valley friends, there was a wider range—a marine worker, two business owners, the barista from the coffee shop. Good people. Just like Champ.

"I'll check it out. As soon as I have my new family member, I'll invite you over for a visit."

"I'll see you at the vet's office, too—right? I told Dr. Cooper you'd be coming in soon. Will it be soon?"

"Absolutely. I'll make a check-up appointment, and hopefully I can make sure he has everything he needs before coming home. This list will be really helpful. Don't want to forget anything!"

"I can't wait to meet him, Kevin!

As they parted ways, Kevin realized—that's the first time Champ actually said my name.

Chapter 32

It wasn't a him, it was a her. Kevin realized he'd been referring to the unknown cat as a "he" all along, but it was a "she" he brought home.

Molly was a five-year-old gray cat with light blue eyes. Her elderly owner Max had become increasingly ill and was finally forced to move to a nursing facility with a firm "no pets" policy. The volunteer at the shelter said Max was heartbroken, but had no other options. He'd already checked with a few distant family members and a few younger friends who all declined. The shelter promised to find Molly a loving home.

Kevin decided he'd find a way to make periodic visits with Molly to the nursing home. Even if he'd have to cajole someone into bending the rules.

Before taking her from the shelter, he visited a few days in a row to spend time with her, letting her sit on his lap as he gently stroked her fur to discover her likes and dislikes. Running his index finger slowly from her nose to the top of her head—like. Stroking either of her sides—dislike.

On the day Molly would arrive at Coastal View, he worked from home to allow plenty of time. He arrived at the shelter with a carrier, then followed his usual routine, letting Molly sit on his lap. When she relaxed, he coaxed her into the carrier. She seemed momentarily confused, followed by slightly frantic. Eventually she stretched out on the floor of the carrier.

"What a gentle girl you are," Kevin said.

"She really is." Cecilia, the 50-something woman with the long gray pony-tail and tie dye shirt had taken a stronger than usual liking to Molly. She knew Kevin was a good fit judging from the days he came in to give Molly the time she needed to connect. "Based on her demeanor, I think she's already bonded with you."

Kevin hoped so. He'd already told Kia about the new member of *their* family, and knew he'd take Molly for a visit back east when the timing was right.

He tried not to swing the carrier too much as he walked. Molly remained settled, and he didn't want to cause added anxiety. The separation from her owner must have been as painful for her as it was for Max. Rather than put Molly through added stress with a vet visit at another time, he'd set up the checkup on the same day.

The bell jingled as he opened the door to the office, Champ waiting behind the desk with the receptionist.

"This is Kevin and Molly," he announced.

"Champ has been waiting for you both," the young, blonde receptionist said and then lowered her voice, "I think he's excited to meet Molly."

"Just Molly? Aren't you excited to see me, Champ?"

"I already know you," he said, eyes fixed on the carrier.

"OK, I guess I'm second place now. I get it. Molly is pretty cute."

Kevin put the carrier down, opened the door and held his hands in place to scoop her up. She stretched to look around the room, curious about the new setting. After a minute, she settled down again on Kevin's lap as he gently stroked the area from her nose to her head.

Champ sat down, leaving one chair open between them. "You're nice. You're a nice girl," he said in a kind of sing-song voice that sounded like a purr.

When it was time for the appointment, Kevin looked at Champ and asked if he'd like to join them.

"You'll have to ask Dr. Cooper. That's up to her," he said, looking at the floor.

"Of course, Champ can join us, he'll be assisting me," Dr. Cooper said, her brown hair now slightly out of the bun that was neatly arranged when she'd arrived that morning. She gestured to the first of three doors adjacent to the receptionist's desk. Inside, there was a small table. Dr. Cooper followed, tablet in hand.

"Champ is like our cat whisperer around here," she said. "When there's something going on that we can't figure out, I ask him to spend some time with them and give me a diagnosis. I keep telling him we're going to start calling him Dr. Champ."

"I need to go to school for that," he said, but straightened his stooped position slightly.

Kevin was glad to see Champ was valued at his job.

Dr. Cooper was thorough. Molly was healthy, and by all appearances, one happy cat. The vet was amazed she wasn't exhibiting more anxiety after the separation from Max.

Kevin settled up the bill in the waiting room while Champ chatted with Molly through the carrier.

As he put away his credit card, he turned toward Champ. "When do you want to come over for a visit? Saturday afternoon—1:00?"

"Yes. I'll be there."

And this time, Champ was definitely smiling.

Chapter 33

Granston was 10 minutes early. He sat in the small reception area, waiting to meet with Bill Rafferty—someone who placed great value on punctuality. He also placed great value on loyalty and devotion to duty. And attention to detail.

Today, Granston would give his usual updates and focus on his actions. He had a list inside his leather portfolio, which he recited in his mind:

1. Security checks continue—no issues.

2. Positive discussions with residents at New Year's Day Brunch; one resident requested additional attention after a family issue when the house was vacant.

3. Closer scrutiny on one of the residents (stressing there were no issues, merely precautionary based on the residents' behavioral traits).

4. FBI request--standard questioning of residents to gather any observations. Tomorrow, will beginning prep sessions with residents. Will offer to drive residents to sessions.

He originally considered starting with the last update, but ultimately decided his boss wouldn't focus on any of the remaining items. He spent some time working and reworking the list for optimal presentation. He shouldn't have wasted his time.

Once seated in the heavily wood-adorned, dark office, Rafferty held up his index finger to indicate a short wait, then tapped a bit on his laptop. He moved over to sit on the edge of the desk.

"Good morning, Granston—what's happening with the FBI?"

So much for his carefully curated list. He leaned forward.

"To gain any potential observations by residents on the fronting street, the FBI will conduct standard questioning sessions over the next week. Tomorrow, I'll begin a casual prep session with each resident to ensure they know what to expect. The location of these sessions is to be determined, but I've offered the sheriff's department offices. I'll also offer transportation for each resident to remind them of our prep and answer any questions on the way."

Granston took a breath, realizing he'd forged through without a pause. He wondered if Rafferty was listening—he was still looking out the window without response. After an uncomfortable silence, he turned.

"I'm not happy with the FBI's involvement, but there's nothing to be done. I suppose you worked your law enforcement network?"

Granston nodded somberly.

"I can't begin to tell you how important Coastal View is for the company's future. And your future, too. I expect that within the year I'll be offering you a full-time position to oversee security for Rafferty Enterprises—with locations across the country. You'd be responsible for strategy, training, recruitment. Much more detail to follow, including a sizeable, sizeable pay increase."

There had been subtle suggestions of this before, but Granston thought the possible expansion might include the same duties at one or two nearby locations.

"I appreciate your confidence."

"Let's keep an eye on the future while dealing with the present. I don't want this to get out of hand. Anything more?"

Granston launched seamlessly into the rest of the list, trying to remain professional and focused as the phrase "sizeable increase" bounced in his head. Once he stepped into the elevator and began the decent, he allowed himself to view the big picture. The FBI investigation would make or break his career with Rafferty Enterprises. He reached the lobby and strode outside, the unmistakable scent of pine and the razor-sharp cold hitting him at once, a sudden slap in the face. And in that moment he knew—he would do whatever it took to ensure his future.

Chapter 34

Kevin tried not to take it personally. He always tried not to take it personally. The interview schedules were out, and he was first on the list. Maybe the FBI didn't even know what he looked like, but his heart seemed to stop for a moment each time this happened.

He grew up in a mostly black community of skilled blue-collar workers, business owners, and professionals. The first time he felt the anxiety he was nine. His cousin Melvin was halfway through high school and finished for the summer. His uncle and father's families seemed to merge on weekends, and especially during the long summer break.

It was Friday. The traditional day for Chinese carryout from Number One and just a 10-minute drive away. Kevin ordered Chicken Chow Mein. He remembered because that was what he always ordered. After that day, he never ordered it again.

Melvin offered to pick up the food, asking if Kevin wanted to go. They were in the midst of an especially long Philadelphia heat wave.

His cousin drove his 1968 Mustang, restored by Melvin and his father. A project still underway since some of the upholstery was worn and even torn in spots—not straight lines, but more like lightning bolts. Kevin remembered those torn seats clearly. He remembered nearly everything about that interior. As usual, the air conditioning wasn't working, so all the windows were down and warm air circulated to Kevin in the backseat.

The food sat on the floor next to him in a big plastic bag. He could smell the spices and sauces, and was certain he could pick out just the scent of his Chicken Chow Mein. Maybe he was like a bloodhound. His father had read him a story about the breed, which had great skills in picking up scents. They could follow scent on a trail for over 100 miles and distinguish each individual scent. Maybe he was the human form of a bloodhound.

He felt the car slow, the cars in the other lane breezing past. "You drive like my mom," Kevin laughed.

Melvin didn't respond. Just kept glancing up, to look in his rearview mirror. That's when Kevin felt the anxiety. Radiating from his cousin to him. And then he heard a siren.

"Oh man," Melvin said, easing to the shoulder.

"What's wrong?"

"It's good, little man. Just take a minute."

But he could hear something different in his cousin's voice.

The police officer appeared at the open window.

"What are you doing around here?" he asked.

"Just picking up some Chinese, officer. My cousin and me."

The office glanced in the back at Kevin.

"Do you live around here?"

"Yes, sir. My parents are over on Oxford. Enjoying my summer break."

The officer paused, looking back to Kevin again.

"I need to see your license, registration, insurance."

"Here's my license. The other paperwork is in the glove box, sir." He reached over slowly and pulled out a plastic sleeve. "Both in here, officer."

The officer didn't move. "Take them out."

Melvin seemed to struggle getting the documents out of the holder. Kevin watched the officer shift from one foot to another. The Chicken Chow Mein smell almost overpowering.

"Stay here," the officer said, heading back to his car.

"What happened?" Kevin asked. "Were you speeding?"

"We don't ask. Just a few more minutes, Kevin."

The smell from the food filled every inch of the car—heavy, thick. He didn't feel hungry anymore. And he felt less and less hungry as time went on, sweat forming on his face and neck. He saw the same on the back of Melvin's head—drops of sweat streaming down onto his blue t-shirt.

"It's hot."

"I know, buddy. Just a little longer."

Finally the officer returned.

"I need you to step out of the car, keep your hands where I can see them."

"Am I being arrested?"

"There's an issue with your insurance—according to the card it's expired."

"Oh, I'm sorry about that. I can get—probably in my wallet."

"Step out. We'll straighten this out at the precinct."

"My cousin—he's only nine."

"I'll call someone."

Melvin was out of the car, his hands behind his back. Kevin could see his face, sweat streaming. There were two metal clicks and his cousin shut his eyes.

"Melvin?" Kevin called out from the back, his voice cracking. "Melvin?"

"It's gonna be OK, buddy. We'll wait for your mom or dad—right officer?"

"Number?"

His father and uncle were there so quickly, Kevin couldn't help thinking they could have been pulled over for speeding. There was a brief exchange between his uncle, Melvin, and the officer. Low voices. Then the officer led Melvin back to his car, the light still flashing.

"Come on son," his father said, opening the back door. "You want to grab that food?"

"Dad?"

"Yes, Kevin?"

"Is it OK if I don't eat it?"

Chapter 35

Granston arrived five minutes early and Kevin was waiting.

"Good morning," he said, getting into the passenger's side. "I guess it's as good a day as any to meet with the FBI." Injecting some humor might diffuse his growing sense of dread.

"Just a conversation. You might be a witness without knowing it."

Kevin nodded. He looked down and tried to inconspicuously brush some of Molly's hair from his pants.

"It's simple. Just what we talked about," Granston said. "Give them your answers, but no need to elaborate. Expanding outside the focus area tends to send folks down a rabbit hole. A rambling rabbit hole."

Just riding in a law enforcement vehicle with a uniformed officer set Kevin on edge. He struggled to find a comfortable position. He tried leaning forward, shifting to the side. Sitting back. Still, he knew his position in the seat wasn't the problem. He'd considered other transportation options, but it was a long ride on his bike and he didn't want to look disheveled for the interview. Neat, professional, trustworthy—that's the image he wanted to maintain.

Riding with Granston had one perk. The visitors' lot was some distance away, with "law enforcement" only spaces right up front.

"OK if I walk in with you? I can at least point you in the right direction."

Was there a choice? Kevin nodded. The two entered the plain, dark red brick building, pulling one of the glass doors and stepping into a security screening area. On the other side, Kevin collected his phone, wallet, and coins, following Granston to the reception desk.

"Good morning. Would you call Agent Ferguson and let him know Kevin Thompson is here for him? Well head up to the fourth floor to meet him."

On the elevator, Granston caught Kevin's eye. "Answer questions. Don't elaborate. Just a conversation."

Agent Ferguson was waiting when the doors opened, and after introductions, Granston pointed to the small waiting area. "I'll be there waiting when you're finished."

***

The return drive was easier, even in a law enforcement vehicle. Just 45 minutes with Agent Ferguson, and the first 10 minutes were casual conversation. He didn't expect questions up front about why he'd moved to Coastal View, but the agent worked the inquiries in so seamlessly, he almost thought they were chatting in a coffee shop. As he left the room, the agent shook his hand, gave him a card, and said, "give me a call if anything else comes to mind." Sounded like an ending.

Kevin picked off another piece of cat hair. "I hope my cat's hair isn't all over your interior," he said.

"Didn't realize you had a cat," Granston said. "The first pet in Coastal View…or does Champ have a pet or two. Hard to know with that one."

That one. Kevin immediately felt protective.

"Actually, Champ was really helpful when I decided to adopt a pet. Even brought Molly—that's her name—her first present."

Even from the side, Kevin saw Granston's skeptical smirk. Indication there was more information he wouldn't share. The rest of the drive continued with safe conversation about the expansion of Coastal View.

"Appreciate the lift!" Kevin said, as they pulled in front of his house.

"No problem at all."

"Also appreciate the advice. Really kept me from going down that rabbit hole you mentioned."

And when Kevin was nearly out of the car, Granston offered one more piece of advice. "Just a word of warning. I'd definitely be careful around Champ."

With one foot out of the car already he just nodded, fighting his desire to get back inside and continue the conversation. He was too relieved to argue.

Chapter 36

Almost finished. Evan's interview had gone well this morning. Now he'd make the roundtrip drive a second time, since Champ's time was late afternoon.

Tomorrow, Lou and Loretta would be interviewed together, just after Ruth's appointment. Granston had hoped to talk with Ruth on the way, but Lou had offered a ride.

Still, he'd have an opportunity talk more with the resident who needed extra attention from a security standpoint. Realistically, though he'd have a hard time having any conversation with this passenger.

Granston's first observation—Champ was wearing a black suit and his hair was combed. So out of character, but the FBI agent didn't know him well enough to realize the transformation.

He slid into the seat, his clip-on tie nearly disconnecting.

"Good afternoon, Champ."

The passenger was struggling with the seatbelt.

"Need some help?"

There was no response, but the metallic click finally signaled success.

"Just remember what we talked about before. Tell them anything you remember. Answer the questions one-by-one."

He didn't feel the need to remind Champ about limiting detail. The agent would be lucky to get more than a nod.

As he feared, the drive continued in silence, despite his best attempts. Granston accepted defeat and turned the volume up on a local talk radio program. Today's topic—major waterfront clean-up for the spring. The host interviewed a marine environmental expert, and then an animal rights activist who talked about the impact of plastics on marine life. He was just glad they'd moved on from discussing the missing girl.

Granston followed the same procedure, accompanying Champ into the building. Although Kevin and Evan had instinctively placed their items on the belt without prompting, Champ just stood by the guard.

"Please place all items in your pocket in the bowl. And here's another bowl for your belt."

He slowly followed the commands then stood in front of the metal detector. "Sir, please walk through."

Champ showed no signs of moving.

"It's OK, Champ—just walk through," Granston coaxed. *It shouldn't be so hard.*

He took a few awkward steps under the metal bars, then stopped.

"Please pass though, sir. Keep coming."

Granston gestured with his hand for Champ to take the last few steps, then another gesture to indicate he needed to pick up his personal items.

Agent Ferguson was waiting when the elevator doors opened on the fourth floor. He'd considered giving the FBI agent a heads-up that Champ was a little different, but decided to let it play out. Besides, Champ was looking at the ground when Ferguson tried, unsuccessfully to shake his hand.

Granston took a seat in the waiting area. He checked email, the weather, and national news. Eventually, he checked his watch. The interview was running long. At one point, he saw another agent, a female, enter the room. Probably hard to get a full answer out of this subject, even with two qualified, experienced agents.

When Champ emerged, Ferguson looked on edge. "We may be calling you again, to answer additional questions."

A different wrap up than the sessions with Kevin and Evan.

As they stepped into the elevator, Granston felt a sense of relief. He wasn't the only one with questions. Someone else had suspicions about Coastal View's oddest resident.

Chapter 37

The first week in February seemed unusually hopeful. Despite continued gray skies, the weather was nearly 20 degrees warmer than average. Ruth met a friendly young couple who would be moving into a Phase 2 house that spring. And, she'd just received an unexpected raise at work. Evan would certainly call for a celebratory dinner when she told him.

And on her lunch break today, she'd meet with Heritage Hill's Fire Chief. Since her meeting with Father Anthony, her mind was in constant spin like the prize wheel at the annual fair. Except this wheel had only two spaces: *not wanting to know* and *wanting to know*. In her mind she spun the wheel and it alternated spaces. Yesterday, when it landed on *wanting to know*, she immediately called the fire department before she could change her mind.

She was aware the conversation would set off a series of steps, and she committed to continue, whatever the results may be. She'd decided to remove Evan from the equation—she deserved to know the truth. No matter if the relationship continued, or didn't continue, Ruth needed to know for certain. For now and for the future.

Inside, there seemed to be numerous young men her age, all seemingly on a mission to make her comfortable.

"Would you like a coffee?"

"Have a seat over here where it's warm—there's cold air near the door."

"I'll make sure he knows you're here so you don't have to wait."

She probably attended school with some of them.

The next one spoke, as though reading her mind.

"Hi Ruth—remember me from Heritage High? I'm not sure if we were in the same classes, but I think we had some mutual friends. Are you still in touch with Marjorie?"

Ruth brightened at the mention of her friend. "We certainly are—we had lunch together last week."

"Tell her I send my best. It's been awhile since I've ran into her."

"You look incredibly familiar," Ruth said tactfully, even though he didn't, "But I can't match your face to your name."

He laughed. "No worries. Augie—Augie Anderson."

Ruth stood to face him. "Augie—of course I remember you! If I recall correctly, you hold the record for planning the best senior prank ever."

"Guilty!"

That caught the attention of the other fire fighters.

Augie shook his head as they prompted for more.

Ruth laughed. "That's on Augie. Not my story to tell."

Augie looked grateful but the rest kept the pressure on before the door opened and they quickly returned to their work.

Augie made the introduction. "Chief Jackson meet Ruth Sagmire."

"Nice to meet you Ruth—let's go into my office. I have all the records there."

"Good seeing you, Ruth," Augie said.

She gave him a little wave, walking alongside the chief to his office, where he closed the door behind them and gestured to one of the chairs fronting his desk.

A manilla folder was on his desk with paperwork visible. Some hand-written, others typed. He gestured to the chair, then sat down behind the desk.

"I was familiar with the case, of course," he started, "But wanted to be sure I accurately recalled all the details before I spoke with you. Was there something specific you wanted to know?"

Ruth noticed he didn't use the word *fire*. She took a breath.

"I was only 12 when it happened, and no one really shared anything. I suppose they were trying to protect me."

"I can understand that. I have a son about the age you were when the incident occurred, not sure how much I'd want him to know either."

Again, not using the word fire.

"I suppose I could have looked up the information myself. But I didn't."

The chief simply nodded, waiting for her to continue.

She decided to get to the point before she lost her momentum. "No one ever told me what started the fire."

"I see. That's important to you? You're certain?"

"It is," Ruth said softly, all the while thinking his questions might be a bad sign about the cause.

He nodded. "Well, it's all right here, but I'll give you the synopsis. Faulty electrical wiring."

"Faulty electrical wiring of what?"

He looked confused, so she continued. "Was it an appliance? In one of the bedrooms? An appliance left plugged into the outlet?"

He still looked confused, and referred to his paperwork. "Faulty electrical wiring, the house wiring. The fire started downstairs in the center of the house—in the living room. It rose quickly to the second floor, to the bedrooms."

Ruth was momentarily stunned, but had to be sure she wasn't missing something. After all these years.

"Is there a mention of anything plugged into an outlet in the bedroom?"

"Upstairs. Hmmm. Definitely didn't start on the second floor," he kept looking. "In the kitchen, there were some appliances plugged into outlets, and a TV on the left side of the living room," he looked up. "But those appliances weren't at the origination point. Not related."

Ruth's hands were shaking, as she started to cry.

"And you're sure?"

"I'm sure," he said, then looked closer at one of the pages. "Evidence shows the fire started in the left interior wall of the living room and spread rapidly, to some exposed insulation."

Her father did all the repairs in the house—no matter what the fix. The family didn't have money to hire experts.

She had a sudden, clouded memory of him working on wiring. She remembered some of the lights had been flickering on and off around that time. Her mother had even joked that the check for the electric bill must have gotten lost in the mail.

"Are you OK, Ruth? Not what you were expecting?"

She pulled out a tissue and wiped her eyes and cheeks. "It's not what I was expecting."

"I'm sorry, Ruth,"

She looked up. "Oh no—this is not—it's certainly better than I expected. Better than I ever thought. This is a relief. Truly, a relief."

He smiled and nodded. "Do you have any other questions for me?"

She stood and smiled, still wiping away tears. "I just wish I'd come in sooner. Much, much sooner."

Chapter 38

There was another one. After dark. Walking alone. Even by the dim street lights, he could tell she was one of the innocent ones.

He'd done this before. Surprise her from the back. Place the rag with chloroform over her mouth. The grave was already prepared. Just another two feet to dig.

Yet he remained in the shadows. The other girl. The questions. The town was already buzzing about the FBI's involvement. This girl needed to be saved, but the time wasn't right.

As she walked further and further down the street, he started to cry. Failure. He could have saved her. And now she would become like so many others.

He told himself to be happy that he'd already saved some. And they didn't even thank him.

Chapter 39

Molly was secure in her carrier as Kevin walked out the door, down the steps, and headed to the back of Coastal View. It seemed to rain every weekend, but on this Saturday, the sun was out and the forecast clear for the next two days. The temperatures hovered near freezing, but his faced soaked in the sun's warmth.

It had taken some convincing, but Champ finally agreed to let Kevin (and Molly) visit. He'd visited Kevin's house on several occasions now.

He wondered if anyone had actually been inside Champ's house. Possibly Ruth on her cake delivery. Maybe Granston, who seemed convinced there was something sinister going on. And surely Mr. Champion had visited his son, although Champ never mentioned his father during their conversations.

Kevin wanted Champ to know he had at least one person he could trust in his life. One person he could rely on, when needed. Kia saw her Kev in that role. And he knew how important that role was to her.

As much as he tried to believe his reasons for the visit were purely altruistic, there was a sense of curiosity he couldn't shake. What would the house look like inside? What kinds of objects did Champ surround himself with? Would there be pictures? What state would he find the house in?

Champ was in a state of general disarray whenever Kevin saw him. He steeled himself, expecting the house to fit the same description.

Inside, the first thing he noticed was the smell. Something old. Musty. Unpleasant. But the interior looked relatively clean, although not organized. Collections of things. Rocks, some medium-sized, others small stones, on the bookshelf. Small animal figurines that Kevin realized were grouped in pairs. An elephant with a rhino. A bear with a sheep. A giraffe with a tiger. Maybe Champ's view of utopia.

On the top shelf, next to more rocks, was a single picture.

"That's a great picture—you and your parents?" Kevin asked.

"In Arizona," he said, suddenly animated. "I got to ride a horse and feed the donkeys."

"That's cool! Summer vacation?"

"In the dessert. We went for three weeks," Champ frowned. "But my father only went for one week. My mother and I had fun."

Kevin noted he didn't mention his father and fun in the same sentence. He'd heard from Loretta that Mr. Champion was a gruff man.

"You must miss her. My mother is gone and I think about her all the time."

Champ picked up the picture and looked at it closely, held it against his chest for the briefest of moments and then suddenly returned it to the shelf. "I'm sorry you lost your mother, Kevin." Champ quickly turned his attention to the carrier. "Can Molly explore?" he asked. "There's no food or other stuff on the floor. I used the vacuum." He pointed to a small floor sweeper model in the corner.

"Of course she can explore," Kevin said. "I think she knew we were coming to visit. You're her favorite friend."

Champ's face brightened, top to bottom as his smile stretch the furthest Kevin had ever seen. He unzipped the case and Molly exited in one quick leap.

"She's happy!" Champ said. "She likes it here!"

"And here's her favorite toy," Kevin said.

"The one I gave her!" Champ jiggled the feather toward her and she pounced back and forth. "She does like the toy. I knew she would!"

Then with a serious look, he turned toward Kevin. "Do you think purple is her favorite color?"

"Well, she does like the purple feather."

"Maybe she just likes the feather. Maybe she'd like another color feather even better."

"I guess that's possible. What's your favorite color, Champ?"

"Purple. But dark purple. This was the darkest purple feather they had in the store, but I looked for one that was darker."

Kevin realized the rocks on the shelf all seemed to reflect a shade of purple. Some really muted. But now that he was looking for it, he realized why Champ collected those particular rocks.

"OK—I see why you picked your display. All rocks with your favorite color."

"I like rocks, but not as much as I like animals. Did you see my animals? My mother collected them. Me, too. I think my father's gonna collect them."

"I saw them as soon as I walked in. That's a nice display. I like that you've paired them with a friend."

Below the rocks, he saw a series of small boxes, with numbers on the top. Not uniform boxes, but all around the same size. Neatly stacked.

"Is that another collection? Those boxes down there?"

The light from Champ's face fell. "That's private," he said.

"No worries. We all have things that are private."

Champ nodded, keeping his head down and playing with Molly. Kevin hoped his question wasn't going to spoil the visit. As much as he remained curious about the boxes – now even more so – he'd need to find a way to warm the mood again.

"Do you know what Molly really likes?"

Champ looked up but didn't respond. Kevin sat on the other side of Molly, putting her on his lap. She wriggled and moved back to the toy.

"I think she really likes the toy," Champ said, the light on his face rising again.

"Sometimes I think you know her better than I do."

"I just know cats. I know lots of animals, but cats are my favorite."

"She does like it when I run my finger up from her nose like this," Kevin said, leaving her on the floor and crooking his arm around to reach the top of her head and running it down to her nose, Molly softly purring.

"She really does like that," Champ said, talking faster than usual. "Let me try."

Champ repeated the motion, over and over—a magic spell that he didn't want to end. His smile stretching as Molly purred.

"See—you do know things about your cat."

"I guess. I think that's only because you and Molly are teaching me."

"Molly and I are the teachers, right Molly? he asked, tilting his head to the side so he could see her response. "Kevin is our student."

"That sounds about right. Should I call you professor?"

"If I can call you student," Champ laughed.

They sat on the floor together for awhile longer until Kevin noticed the time.

"I've got a call in a half-hour. I guess I'd better start back."

"OK, Champ said. I'll walk with you. I need to get my mail."

"It's a nice day today—lots of sun," Kevin said as he unzipped Molly's carrier for the quick trip home.

"I like the clouds better," he said. "Or the dark. The sun hurts my eyes."

"It's bright today, but not that bright. I think you'll be OK."

"Just a minute—I'll use the bathroom first."

The door shut, and Kevin's attention immediately shifted to the boxes. Before he had time to reconsider, he lifted the lid on the box labeled "1". There were hair clippings inside. Blonde. He quickly opened the box labeled "2"—light brown hair with streaks of brown.

He quickly returned both lids and stacked the boxes, counting. There were eight total. His mouth felt dry, his stomach suddenly unsettled.

The bathroom door opened so suddenly, it banged the wall behind it

"Ready," Champ said, as he pulled on his coat, fastening each toggle.

Kevin quickly zipped Molly back in the case. What could this possibly mean? There was an immediate, horrifying thought. The most obvious explanation. But certainly, there had to be another one. One that didn't make him question everything he thought about Champ.

Chapter 40

The return text from Marjorie was immediate: *He asked about me?* And a second. *Are you sure?*

Ruth had texted her friend about Augie's inquiry at the firehouse.

Definitely!

She felt lighter than she had for as long as she could remember, and wanted to share the joy she felt, especially in light of Marjorie's recent relationship change. Her fiancé had broken up with her on the 23rd of December. Ruth knew because her friend kept reminding her. (Who breaks up two days before Christmas? Did he forget to buy a gift and that was his only way out? Did I do something wrong?)

The texts continued. *Did he ask about other people from school? Just you.*

What's the next step? BEFORE SOMEONE ELSE SNATCHES HIM UP!!!

Ruth laughed. Sounds like it was time for a small reunion. After a few more texts, they had a plan. Majorie would invite a few other friends from school, and Ruth would call the firehouse and invite Augie. She'd find a way to make it sound more spontaneous than it appeared. She'd invite Evan to be polite, but he had a standing appointment with his uncle for the first Friday of the month Marina Club meeting.

She shook her head. Ruth usually went to school gatherings reluctantly, preferring to meet with just one or two friends at a time. And now she was the one who'd suggested it. And was actually looking forward to going.

Marjorie met Ruth a block from the pub so they could walk in together. As expected, Evan would be at his meeting, but would try to stop by after.

"Augie Anderson—wow," Marjorie said, shaking her head as they walked.

"That's the third time you've said his name," Ruth laughed. "Are you making sure you don't forget?"

"But, it's Augie. Seriously! He really was the best-looking guy in school. And the nicest. Those two never combine into one person," she said. "Well, I'm sure you think Evan fits that description as well, right?"

"He does."

"Then you know it's rare. A rare combination in a single guy. And speaking of single, I'm surprised he is—single, that is."

"By all appearances. Unless he has a family stashed away in the woods somewhere."

"Not Augie! Not *my* Augie! Hey—shouldn't you be telling me to pump the brakes a little? He might not be the same guy we knew in high school, and even if he is, that doesn't mean we're a match. Shouldn't you be telling me to slow down?"

Ruth just laughed. Anything seemed possible, and she hoped some of the happiness she'd found would extend to her friend.

The pub was at half capacity when they entered, and even though they were ten minutes early, Augie was already there at the corner of the bar.

"Ladies," he said over the noise. "Nice to see you again, Ruth. And, Marjorie—you're looking better than ever."

"You always were the flatterer, Augie," Marjorie responded. "But I'll take the compliment!"

"I'm just truthful. Scouts honor," he said, holding up a three-finger salute.

"I bet you were an Eagle Scout," she said.

"Guilty," he laughed. "Let's get some seating—bar or table?"

"Table would be better, Ruth said. "We have a few others joining us."

They moved to a table with four chairs, and Augie pulled over three additional seats.

"More?" he asked.

"Perfect for now," Ruth said.

"Let me get the first drink, ladies," he said, waiting for their orders, then heading to the bar.

"Ruth, it's Augie—"

"Anderson! Yes, I know!"

"Is it wrong to say he looks even better? Is even nicer?"

"It's not wrong. After all he's—"

"Augie Anderson," they both said in unison.

"Oh—Augie's here?" Sheree asked, joining the group.

Ruth and Marjorie started laughing.

"Why? What's funny?"

The rest of the group arrived soon after. Light conversation. Current situations. Old school stories. More laughter. Every time Ruth glanced at either Marjorie or Augie, they were looking at one another. Happiness officially achieved.

At one point, Marjorie headed to the lady's room, and Augie leaned over closely.

"Thank you, Ruth—this is great. And, I'm really glad Marjorie is here."

"And the rest of us?"

"Of course," he laughed.

At the moment Augie leaned in to talk to Ruth above the growing noise around them, someone was watching. He'd been walking by the window when he saw the group, and slipped in quickly, moving to a side area where he could take a step back and be hidden, should Ruth look in his direction. He'd only been in place a couple of minutes when he saw the guy touch her shoulder and move in more closely. She was smiling broadly. Maybe the alcohol. Maybe not. He watched closely as she finished her drink and the server brought another.

He'd always thought of her as one of the good ones. One of the young women who others would try to take advantage of, until they were spoiled. But he thought she'd be safe. She'd always seemed guarded. Now he wondered if everything he thought he knew was wrong.

He immediately thought about his mission. The timing wasn't right, but if he waited, she'd be lost.

He'd have to act fast. Follow the plan. Save Ruth.

Chapter 41

Loretta was organizing her bedroom closet. Again. Living in a tiny house had its benefits, as well as its challenges. Space was finite. No spare room closet. No nook under the staircase. No outside storage shed. The loft had a few boxes around the walls, but she liked the area kept open for grandchildren's visits. A cabinet in the corner was filled with a few games, puzzles and books.

She was certain there was a better way to use the available space, and she'd eventually find it. If only kept rearranging.

For reorganizing part 3 (or was it part 4?), Lou added a second rod. She'd already emptied the closet contents onto her bed and was adding her blouses, grouped by color, on the new bottom rod. She was half-way through the job when she heard a thud.

"Lou? Everything OK?"

No response from her husband, who had been reading the local paper and sipping his coffee before she started her project.

"Lou?" She called out, pushing herself up from the floor on her right side, being careful not to further aggravate the bursitis in her left hip.

When she stepped out of the bedroom, she saw her husband sprawled on the floor. "Lou!" She took the briefest of moments to check him – he was breathing – before calling 911. He had a pulse, but it was weak.

The EMTs arrived quickly and even though they spoke with Loretta while they worked on Lou and moved him onto the stretcher, she didn't hear a word they said. Fortunately, Granston had heard the call on his scanner and Kevin saw the flashing lights enter the community. Both men stood outside the crowded house on the front porch. The door open, they listened to every word.

"Loretta, do you want to ride in the ambulance?" Granston asked, after they moved Lou out of the house. "Or you can ride with me."

The words sounded far away. "With Lou," she managed, her tongue sticking to the roof of her mouth, which felt suddenly gummy.

"I'll meet you there," he said, then turned to Kevin. "Would you mind letting everyone know?"

He nodded. "Let me know what else I can do. Keep me updated?"

"As soon as I know something."

The ambulance pulled away, Loretta in the passenger's seat, turning her body quickly to get a view of Lou in the back, her hip throbbing with the sudden twist.

She wasn't thinking about calling their kids. She wasn't thinking about their plans to meet another couple for dinner that night. She wasn't thinking about her bedroom closet.

Granston was in the waiting room with Loretta when the answers came. There were lots of words but she only heard two phrases: Heart attack. Bypass surgery.

She'd already called family members with his help. Loretta pulling up the names - confused and with shaking hands - and Granston placing the calls.

"What did Charlie say? Is he coming? Robert?"

"They're all coming, Loretta."

"Leslie—she's a nurse."

"She's coming."

Loretta kept repeating her daughter's name.

"Leslie, Leslie. I need her."

"She's on her way. Let me get you some water, Loretta—or coffee, tea?"

She looked at him blankly and Granston returned quickly with a bottle of water from the vending machine, unscrewing the lid and placing it in her still shaking hands.

"Take a sip," he instructed. "Now, let's take some deep breaths." He took the first in a series of slow, deliberate breaths, and Loretta followed.

He alternated her between sips of water and deep breaths. Her shaking finally slowed.

Eventually, her daughter Leslie arrived. And then her sons. "What do I do?" Loretta repeated to each as they arrived.

Granston passed the information to them, along with the doctor's name. He gave his business card to each, instructing them to call if they needed anything. He stepped outside the waiting room and into the lobby, and placed a call to Kevin.

"What's his prognosis?"

"No information yet."

"Is there permanent damage to his heart?"

"The nurse mentioned a surgeon would be out to speak to Loretta shortly. But the fact that there's a surgeon coming out at some point…"

"When is the surgery?"

"There was a definite sense of urgency."

When Granston finished the call, he realized Loretta might need to sign consent forms for the surgery. He'd check to see if she had all of Lou's insurance information on hand.

After he confirmed, he thought about staying a little longer, but decided his time would be better spent checking in on everyone at Coastal View—they'd all be worried about Lou. And the FBI investigation already had everyone on edge.

Chapter 42

Kevin made the calls to Ruth and Evan quickly. He decided not to bother Champ at work. When he saw Champ at the mailbox, he pulled on his coat and stepped outside.

"Hey, Kevin," he said with a small wave. "How's Molly?"

"Molly is great. But I wanted to tell you one of our neighbors is in the hospital."

Champ stopped, his shoulders slumped even more forward than usual. "Not Ruth? She isn't sick?"

"No, not Ruth—it's Lou. He had a heart attack."

"Will he die?"

Kevin paused, not sure how to answer.

"The doctors are taking care of him. Loretta is with him."

"I'm glad he's OK, but I'm really glad it's not Ruth. She's young."

Kevin couldn't remember Champ talking about Ruth before, but she had mentioned once that her family had lived next-door to the

Champions. It was logical that the two had known each other for a long time. Or maybe this was part of his social awkwardness.

"Do you want to come to my house later?" Kevin asked. "Ruth and Evan are coming. I thought we could call Granston to find out if there's an update. Or call the hospital."

"Will Molly be there?"

"She will."

"What time should I come?"

Despite the worrisome situation, Kevin couldn't help but smile when he thought about Champ's love for Molly. He definitely had a close connection with her. But what surprised him was the connection, possibly one-sided, to Ruth. He considered mentioning to her, but didn't want her to think there was anything odd about Champ.

And even though he kept pushing the thought away, he just couldn't get those numbered boxes out of his mind.

Chapter 43

The news about Lou hit Evan hard. Just like he liked spending time with his uncle, he felt the same with Lou. Kind-hearted. Gentle, but robust. Funny, but serious when needed. Like his dad. The lack of control he felt when his father died was back. He felt restless and out-of-sorts. Maybe his anxiety about Ruth was adding to his stress.

Since Christmas, he'd felt a building anxiety. He thought he could let it go, never mention to anyone much less Ruth, but it wasn't working. He couldn't remember the last time he'd slept soundly. The last time his mind was completely clear. And he seemed to be paying the price for it physically. Most days, including today, he woke with a headache. His back ached more and more, even though he wasn't doing much physical work at the marina right now. He looked forward to drinking more than he should, and he was taking double the over-the-counter pain medication than the label suggested.

Ruth didn't seem to notice. She always seemed a bit preoccupied herself since they met, and Evan always thought he'd be the one to help her through whatever was causing that preoccupation. She'd always seemed so fragile, so in need of rescuing. After the fire, when he thought about how he could live in a world where his father didn't, he thought about Ruth. If she was able to move forward with her life after losing all of her family, how could he not move forward with his life? She gave him a strength of sort. Maybe he wanted to return the favor. To give her the strength she'd given him.

Now Evan doubted he was capable of helping her. He wasn't as strong as he thought, or maybe the secret was draining him, little by little. The secret that he knew, once exposed, would drive her away.

How could she ever understand his near obsession with her? The newspaper articles about the fire he collected. The printed pictures from her social media. His constant worry about how she was living her life without her family.

How could she understand that the reason he moved back to Heritage was not just about helping his aunt and uncle? Their request was an answer to his plan. He wanted to move back to save Ruth.

Chapter 44

Just inside the entrance of Municipal General, he could smell the same lemonish solution that was the hallmark of every hospital, and other care facilities. Kevin wondered if those places actually cleaned continuously, or if they pumped it through the HVAC air flow system just to give visitors a positive impression. The clean scent transported him to his last visit with Kia. He missed her. Did all adult twins feel the same separation anxiety?

To others, Kevin was the best of the pair. He had a fun childhood. Rode his red ten-speed up and down the streets of his neighborhood. Played baseball from t-ball and through high school JV and Varsity. Took piano and later trumpet lessons. He finished college and secured a job in his field out on the west coast. And he bought his own home. Signs of success. Really, Kevin knew, those were just signs of independence, not of success.

Kia was pure of heart, selfless. She cared more about others. And by her example, she was forcing Kevin to face some not-so-nice things about himself. Like, why didn't he tell his west coast friends about Kia? They knew he had a sister, but he'd never said more. He'd always felt proud of Kia, of every small step forward. But maybe there was a part of him that felt something else.

Evan requested the room number and passed out visitor stickers to Ruth and Kevin. Lou was on the third floor and permitted only one visitor at a time. They'd coordinated the time, so Loretta could have lunch in the cafeteria with her children to discuss next steps.

The three made their way on the elevator. Kevin had invited Champ, who asked, "Just you and me?" When he mentioned Evan and Ruth would be going he said, "That's too crowded." And even though Kevin assured them Evan's uncle was lending them his car, and there was plenty of room, Champ just shook his head.

They were seated in the lounge when Loretta appeared, her eyes sunken and hair matted like she'd slept overnight in the room (she had).

"It's so good to see all of you," she said, her eyes filling with tears. Ruth rose and gave her a hug, and the others did the same.

"How is he today?" Ruth asked softly.

"He's good. Making progress. His medical team – they have teams now, not just one doctor – said he's making faster progress than they expected. He's still my strong-as-an-ox guy, my Louie" she said, her voice breaking as she said his name. "I guess I'll go downstairs, if you're ready to visit. I don't want to keep you three too long."

"We've got the rest of the day, Loretta," Kevin said. The others nodded. "Nothing on our calendars but visiting Lou. Thought we'd each take a half-hour, then keep repeating as long as you like."

"I'm grateful. Those three half-hour visits will be long enough. We're looking at some options for rehab—just to get him ready to come home. Want to make sure we pick the right place."

"Don't rush on our account, Loretta," Evan said. "We really don't have anywhere to go, or anywhere we'd rather be."

Ruth looked over and smiled at Evan. He always knew how to bring comfort.

Loretta nodded. "You've got my cell number?" she asked, holding up her phone.

"We all have it," Ruth responded. "Try to relax with your family."

As she stepped out of the room, Evan spoke first. "I'll take the first visit if that's OK?"

Ruth and Kevin nodded, not knowing they were both grateful someone else was going in first. They had no idea how different Lou might look.

Their fears weren't necessary. Lou smiled and straightened himself up a bit in the bed when Evan entered. His face was drawn and paler, but overall looked much better than expected for a man who just had major surgery.

"You're a sight for sore eyes, Evan! I wish the circumstances were better. All I can offer you is a dish of sugar free green gelatin with some chopped peaches."

"All good," Evan laughed. "I guess Loretta's not smuggling in any of her cookies, or cakes?"

"Got me on this daggone low-fat diet. Heart healthy is what they call it. Bland is what I call it. Chicken broth. Who eats that? Might as well give me a stalk of celery."

"If they offer you the celery, take it. At least you could chop it up with your plastic knife and make the broth a little better," he smiled.

Lou laughed, then held his chest. "I hope I'm allowed to laugh. The folks here, nice as they are, act like I'll break in two. They don't know how strong I am."

"Isn't laughter supposed to be the best medicine?"

"And good for the soul. Yeah—I think it's OK for me to laugh."

"We're just glad you're doing so well, Lou. They stitched you back up and with a little rest and rehab, you'll be back to the old Lou."

"Oh, I think they have a higher goal. Some Lou hybrid. Even stronger. Loretta's already talking about making her recipes healthier. About us taking a walk every day. Going to the gym."

"I like it. Lou 2.0."

"I think Loretta was tired of Lou 1.0."

"I doubt that," Evan said. "I just think she wants you to be around for a long, long time. Growing old together."

Evan had a sudden vision of two elderly people, taking a walk hand-in-hand out the gates of Coastal View and down the sidewalk, trees just starting to bloom. Maybe they weren't Lou and Loretta.

"It sure is a surprise to see you here," Lou said. "I've been thinking about my young neighbors. How's everyone?"

"You can ask Ruth and Kevin yourself. They're in the waiting room."

"What—tell them to come in. Oh, yeah. Forgot that doggone one visitor at a time rule. I suppose they think people will start a party in here."

"You know we Coastal View people are big partiers," Evan laughed.

"I would expect people who'd willingly move to a grave yard are a fairly quiet lot, don't you think?"

The visit continued so pleasantly that Evan nearly forgot he was on the clock. He was a couple minutes over his time when he checked.

"Time for your next visit," he said. "I can't keep you all to myself."

"Especially Lou 2.0. As it turns out, he's an even happier fellow. Maybe not as happy about the exercise and the food plan, but happy about life."

Ruth followed as the next visitor, and finally Kevin. Evan was glad he and Ruth would have some time together in the waiting room, but right after Kevin left, Loretta and her daughter Leslie appeared.

"Kevin just went back," Ruth said. "You don't need to rush."

"I told her," Leslie said. "But she can't be away from dad for long. I'm grateful you filled in to give her some time with us."

"Our pleasure," Ruth said.

"You two should probably know that I gave him a nickname and he's now referring to himself as Lou 2.0," Evan said.

"That's perfect," Leslie said. "The grandkids will love it!"

"Truly, he looks so healthy," Ruth said. "Looks like he could walk out of the hospital with us and go back home."

"He's making great progress," Loretta said. "And we've found the best rehab for him over in Middleton."

"Great to hear it," Evan said. "That's a bit of a drive for you, Loretta —almost an hour?"

She nodded. "It is. But only 10 minutes from Leslie's. She wants me to stay with her while Lou's in rehab."

"Makes sense," Evan said. "But don't get too comfortable in all that extra space. We don't want you and Lou moving away."

The plan made sense. She'd share the visits to the rehab with her daughter and son-in-law. Spend more time with her grandchildren. The house was near a large state park, where she could take a quiet morning walk before the rehab's visiting hours.

Loretta's only reservation was one she wouldn't share--that opened back door on Christmas Eve. A ghostly presence that wasn't so ghostly. And if it was true, what did that mean for Michael? That he was no longer in treatment? That he would repeat the same destructive behaviors? As much as she tried to apply logic, the whisper of uncertainty filled her mind. Clouded her reasoning. Quickened her heart. Even with the new worries of Lou's health and future, that long familiar narrative would not be silenced.

Chapter 45

He always followed the plan. Except when he didn't.

He was breaking a primary rule. He had a connection to this one. Even if she saw him nearby, no suspicions would be raised. Even if he approached her in view, she wouldn't be scared.

He shook his head. No need to change that part of the plan. When the time came, and it was coming soon, he would come from behind —like the others.

But today was not the day. So he would follow her, staying out of view like a spy on a mission. He wanted to know more about her habits. He followed a safe distance behind, watching her pause to look in the local clothing store window. Watching her stop on the sidewalk to talk to the elderly woman who worked at the diner. He heard them laugh. He couldn't see her face, but he knew she was smiling. She didn't always smile, which made her smile even brighter when she did.

She continued up the sidewalk, slowing at the park and peering around the big oak tree with roots that pushed up the edge of the sidewalk. What did she see?

She took a step forward into the grass, then stooped down. He moved a few steps to the side for a better view. Her arm was outstretched. He followed the line of her hand forward and saw an orange-colored cat. She stretched her arm a little further and the cat retreated. Bolted. The cat thought she was too friendly.

When they first met, she was shy. Now she was brighter and bolder, but not in a good way. He liked her before. Now she was becoming like all the others.

She stood up and brushed her pants, continuing down the path that led her from work to home. The sun emerged from a dark cloud as she made the final turn. And just as the sun dipped back inside its cloud cocoon, she made the final turn into Coastal View.

Chapter 46

Granston was on his way up to the third floor of Municipal General when he nearly ran into Loretta. As the elevator doors opened, Loretta rushed in just as Granston rushed out.

"Oh, Granston," she said looking surprised. "I nearly knocked you over I was in such a hurry. I'm always in a rush these days."

"Everything OK? Is Lou alright?"

"Oh yes, she said, moving to the side so others could access the elevator. "My son is in there now, so I'm headed downstairs for a cup of coffee."

"Do you want company?"

The cafeteria had the two selections of coffee—caf and decaf. Both filled their cardboard cups with the full-strength option.

Loretta stirred in some cream. "Oh, that's dark. Let me add some more."

"Makes you wonder how long that coffee's been sitting here."

Granston pulled out his credit card quickly to pay for both cups at the register, and Loretta didn't argue. "Thank you. I was ready to insist, but realized I left my purse upstairs in Lou's room."

"It's the detective instinct," he laughed. "Do you have time to sit?"

"Just for a few minutes," she said. "My kids keep telling me I need to slow down."

"They don't want to see their mom get sick, too. I've seen that in a lot of families. The caretaker doesn't take care of themselves."

"My kids keep reminding me," she sighed. "I actually did want to talk to you about something—I'm glad I ran into you. I've had something on my mind, something we talked about before, and I thought you might be able to help."

"Of course, Loretta—whatever you need."

"Last time we talked I mentioned my worries about the house. Christmas Eve. The back door left unlocked."

"I remember."

"I just can't seem to shake the feeling that someone was in the house. Maybe I'm just overly fixated on this. Am I going crazy?"

"No, Loretta. I actually do think there's a good chance someone was in your house that day. Your instincts may be right."

"Oh?"

"I wasn't sure if I should mention, but I saw Champ walk around to the back of your house the other day. I thought I should investigate a little further, and when I came around to the back, he actually had his hand on the back door knob."

"Champ?"

"Of course he was startled when I saw him and didn't say anything. I wasn't thinking of what you told me about Christmas Eve. I had a quick thought that maybe you'd asked him to check the doors, to make sure they were all locked."

"And you're sure it was Champ?"

"No doubt. He looked straight at me before he left."

"Champ…"

"Did you ask him?"

Loretta tilted her head to the side. "Ask him?"

"Did you ask Champ to check the house? Check the doors?"

"I didn't. But maybe he took it on himself. Maybe his way of trying to help out."

"Maybe."

"As it turns out, we're not going to be back home for some time. My daughter already returned to pack some clothes for me. Lou should be transitioning to a rehab any day now. It's a highly recommended place near my daughter so I'll be staying with her."

"Sounds like an excellent plan," he said. "Especially because it's a good place. That's the most important thing."

"We were fortunate to get a bed there. I'm relieved, but I've got that nagging feeling about the house."

"Don't worry about it at all. Just put it out of your mind. I'll keep an even closer eye on the house."

"I thought I'd give you a key," Loretta said. "Check it every few days to make sure nothing's out of ordinary?"

"Happy to do it. I'll even water your plants, flush your toilets, and run your water so the lines don't freeze up."

"Hadn't even thought about those things, but that would be a big help. I just have some herbs growing in small pots in the garden window over the sink—help yourself to any fresh herbs you like."

He laughed. "Maybe some fresh oregano will improve the taste of my canned spaghetti and frozen lasagna."

When they returned up to the third floor, Granston spent a few minutes visiting with Lou. In the lobby, Loretta pulled a key from the coin compartment in her wallet.

"Thank you, Granston. This will help me—at least one less thing to worry about."

In the lobby, he passed through the double doors and out into nearly full sun. Coastal View would remain safe and secure.

Chapter 47

Evan had been thinking a lot about the box. It was an old shoe box and if he remembered correctly, it once held his winter boots. The box was smashed on one corner, so the lid didn't fit right. He kept a large, thick rubber band around it to keep the contents from spilling out.

The contents. He thought about his mother or siblings discovering the contents. What would they think? What if Ruth discovered the contents?

It seemed more likely that Ruth could inadvertently discover the list. He couldn't even remember why he made the list in the first place, so he destroyed the physical copy he'd printed to keep with the rest of his "important papers" like is birth certificate and social security card. He still needed to delete the file from his computer. The fact that he'd cataloged the items in a document seemed disturbing, even to him.

Fire Box Contents:

1. Herald article the day after the fire

2. Dad's watch

3. Dad's obituary

4. Sagmire family's obituaries

5. Herald article two days after the fire, with two pictures: dad in uniform and Sagmire family, including Ruth

6. Herald article three weeks after the fire with updates

7. The town's online newsletter "comings and goings" column announcing Ruth had set up permanent residence with her aunt

8. Instagram photo of Ruth, with three girlfriends

9. Instagram photo of Ruth with prom date "Davey"

10. Instagram photo of Ruth in her cap and gown, with a friend

A single item—certain single items--would present a logical answer. Any, even all, newspaper articles about the fire. His father's watch and obituary. All the other items were problematic, although it could be worse. He'd found other pictures, but after those first three, he worried his research was moving toward an obsessive. So he stopped.

When he packed up and moved to his aunt and uncle's house, he purposely left the box behind. His aunt was known as a snooper, finding every gift her husband bought her—no matter how carefully hidden. Living with her confirmed this for Evan. If he left a receipt on the counter, she'd scrutinize it. *You can buy shaving lotion online—*

it's cheaper than the drug store. Oh, I see you went to the diner at noon yesterday. Alone?

No, the box would remain where it was. Hidden in the back of a closet with boxes of photo albums. On his Christmas visit, he'd planned to shred the contents with the few exceptions that wouldn't cause any concern. So now the box sat. Still intact.

Before Christmas, he'd invited her to join him in the spring, so she could meet his family. And now he'd need to disinvite her.

Chapter 48

For some time, Ruth watched her relationship with Evan as an outsider. Like a third person who always considered the impact of her secret. The merry-go-round of their life together kept going round and round, waiting for her to jump aboard. Instead, she stood outside the safety line, watching each turn. Feeling anxious when the ride shifted to a higher rate of speed. When the secret became a shadow, she jumped aboard. Her body finally in rhythm with the tempo of the ride. Until suddenly, the ride slowed.

Little things. He took a longer time to answer texts. Spent more time at work. Seemed distracted at dinner.

He'd always reached for her hand first. But now she found herself reaching for his. When she leaned her head on his shoulder, instead of his shoulder relaxing, she felt stiffness.

This morning, when she envisioned herself on the merry-go-round she saw Evan in a new place. Before, he was riding the black horse, painted with a ring of purple flowers around his neck. Now she saw him standing in her old spot--behind the safety line.

It had been some time since he'd mentioned a trip back home with Ruth. Something he anticipated, but filled Ruth with dread. She no longer feared the visit, and in fact, welcomed it. But Evan hadn't mentioned it since December.

The sun was starting to set as Ruth walked toward the diner. She could see the light reflected from above, brighter than usual. Tonight, she'd ask Evan when she could meet his family.

A bold move. Bold moves were long overdue in her life. Had she ever had them? Before the fire. Not after. Ever since her meeting with the Fire Chief, she'd been thinking about what else the fire took from her. She'd mourned the loss of her family for a long time. So much that she didn't think about the other losses. Her right to a happy life. Her absence of guilt. Her boldness. If she'd possessed the boldness earlier, if she'd grabbed it and held onto it, and used it, she would have met with Father Anthony and the Fire Chief sooner.

Boldness. Ruth's new creed.

She felt the rush of instant warmth when she opened the heavy diner door, and she stamped off the slushy grime from the sidewalk onto the mat. The smell of meatloaf (tonight's special) wafted through the place, and she glanced back to the area they both favored. No Evan yet, but she moved toward the one empty booth. Their usual server Tina approached while Ruth was still removing her coat.

"Pinot Grigio?"

"Yes, please."

The waitress pointed to the other side of the table. "We've got that craft beer he likes."

"Sure—thank you."

Ruth rubbed her hands together to warm them a bit. No snow expected in this week's forecast, but the dampness and dip in temperature certainly made it feel like snow was possible. The forecasts had been so off this year, maybe she should delete her weather app altogether.

Evan arrived at the same time as the drinks. She noted that he didn't lean in to kiss her cheek before he sat on the opposite side, although that was likely out of consideration for Tina who was waiting to place the beverages on the table.

"One of you read my mind," Evan said, smiling.

"That was Tina," Ruth said. "I just approved her suggestion."

"Thanks, Tina," he said taking a sip of equal parts foam and beer.

"I know you both know the menu," she said. "Not rushing you…"

"Oh, I think we're ready," Evan said. "At least I am."

Ruth nodded. "Meatloaf for me."

"Same."

"Are we getting set in our ways?" Ruth asked to no response.

Evan was checking his phone, spending a minute reading, texting, then reading again. "Looks like I'm headed back home for a couple days," he said to Ruth, continuing before she interrupted. "Just a short trip. Need to take care of something for my mother."

"Everything OK? That seems sudden."

"More about the timing. Good time to take a few days off, good time for weather conditions. Thought I'd take care of it at Christmas, but you know how that worked out," he frowned.

Ruth thought there was a part of him who was happy he'd missed his trip home because they were able to spend at least part of the day together. Maybe that's just what she hoped.

"Don't worry—we'll still take that trip in the spring. A promise is a promise."

Something about his last comment didn't sit right with Ruth, but his comment was factual. Evan had promised. She hoped he wanted to introduce her to her family, but he didn't mention that. Still, he'd mentioned it before.

"I'm looking forward to it," she said simply.

Evan had felt the color rise up his neck when he'd said the purpose of the trip was to take care of something for his mother. He sipped his beer again, then reached over the table with his palm up. Ruth placed her hand in his. He hoped she hadn't noticed. Evan's skin always flushed when he lied.

Chapter 49

It's all in the spin. Granston already understood the concept of spin, but Bill Rafferty provided a close-up, master's level training in execution. Tiny houses in a graveyard? He'd spun that concept in such a positive light that would-be residents and investors were clamoring for a piece of *the future of housing today*. Rafferty's new tag line.

As Granston stepped back into his boss' office, he lifted his head and threw back his shoulders, just as his mother had taught him and his sister. The look of confidence.

"Always look like you belong," she'd tell them when they visited more affluent relatives in their homes, or accepted dinner invitations at fancy restaurants. All their relatives were more affluent—there wasn't much of a bar since his father disappeared and left the family with nothing but his debts. The worst part—he'd left them vulnerable. Especially his sister.

The brief thought of her tragic tale caused his shoulders to move downward, but he shifted them back again. Today, he wasn't just projecting an image. He had become the image. Successful. Confident.

Rafferty closed his laptop and looked directly at him. "Status?"

"I'm pleased to report there are no security issues. The FBI has what they need. Coastal View is tight as a drum. I've expanded my security checks to the perimeter. One block radius surrounding the community. Residents are now reporting when their homes will be vacant for any length of time."

"Interesting. Did you ask them? Did any see this as an invasion of privacy."

"Resident-initiated."

Rafferty tilted his head, raised his finger to the corner of his mouth. "And so far? No issues when houses were vacant?"

"No issues," he started hesitantly. "Of course, I'm continuing to keep an eye on Champ. He seems to wander a bit." He decided not to share additional information. No need to ripple the currently still waters. Sun was shining. No waves in sight.

The same head tilt. An uncomfortable space of silence, Granston had grown accustomed to when speaking to his boss.

"Under control. Good. Do you know what this means?"

Now Granston titled his head, but remained silent.

"This means you'll need to recruit a new security person."

Granston frowned, then relaxed as he waited for the next line. He knew Rafferty had more to say.

"Time for the next phase of your career."

He knew the offer was coming. Although he still hadn't fully processed what that meant for his life. In a purely logical review, this offer made sense. And career timing made sense as well. Granston was already poised to leave his part-time work at the Sheriff's Department. He knew this next phase would include a huge bump in salary, even though money wasn't a motivator for him. He still lived in the small dwelling passed down from his mother. But there were other motivating factors.

What would this mean for his life mission? A mission he'd established when he was just a young teen. After his sister's tragic life, he'd made a promise to his inconsolable mother. *I'll spend the rest of my life helping people.* And so he would. In fact, he'd be expanding his life mission. Helping more people in more places. His mother would be proud. Time to give his notice to the Department and advertise his current Coastal View job.

His head high, shoulders back, he walked out of the office and pressed the elevator down button. Successful. Confident.

Chapter 50

Kevin had learned a lot about himself lately. Maybe living alone left more time for reflection. He liked some of what he'd learned. Other revelations—not so much. For years, he'd told himself he was just ultra-particular when it came to women. Not about looks or level of success, but about their hearts. More recently he'd realized (or finally admitted) that he was holding them to an impossible standard. Kia.

He himself was learning and growing. Shouldn't the women he dated be permitted the same space? Of course, some were just too far from his values, and he could generally pick up on those clues by the second or third date. Sometimes the first.

For the past month, he'd been seeing someone a couple nights a week for dinner, and sometimes a movie. Tonight they had tickets to the local theater's production of Oscar Wilde's The Importance of Being Earnest.

They. He couldn't remember the last time he was part of a *they*.

He was walking down to Champ's, carrying Molly in the portable crate. She'd been sitting by the door all morning, making him wonder if she was looking for a visit from her friend. He hoped Champ would react well to a surprise visit. His previous visit was arranged in advance. The visit when he saw the numbered boxes with the hair. There could be any number of logical explanations, couldn't there? He pushed it out of his mind. His aunt credited Kevin with the gift of reading people. And his gift told him there was nothing to be concerned about. Champ was decent, although often misunderstood.

He knocked on the front door. No answer. Then, he heard the sound of hard footsteps to his right. Champ was coming from the pet gravesite area.

"Hey Kevin," he shouted, his face lighting up when he saw the cat carrier.

"Molly was missing you. She sat by the door all morning."

"Oh! I'm glad she missed me! That means she's my friend."

"She's definitely your friend, Champ. Sometimes I think she likes you more than she likes me."

Champ unlocked his door. "She likes us both. Don't you, Molly?"

Inside, the place was dark, but neat. Curtains drawn. Blanket folded on the end of the sofa. Numbered boxes with hair on the shelf. He briefly considered asking about the boxes. Asking if Champ had a collection. Next time.

Instead, he sat on the edge of the sofa and opened the carrier. Molly burst out and headed toward Champ, who was already seated on the floor. She settled herself on his lap.

"She rarely sits on my lap," Kevin said. "She really does like you better!"

"No—you just need to sit on the floor. Molly likes it when you come down to her."

"I'll try it," he said looking around. Everything really was in its place. "Your place is so neat—do you have a maid?" he teased.

"No—my mother taught me."

"She did a good job."

"She taught me a lot of things. Everything in its place. Be kind to animals. Do the right thing."

"Your mom sounds like a terrific lady. I bet you miss her."

Champ nodded. "Molly would like her. You'd like her, too."

"I'm sure I would like her."

"How about your mom? Does she teach you things?"

"She taught me a lot. She taught me to always be kind. To help everyone, even if I didn't want to."

"Does she know about Molly?"

"My mom is gone now, Champ—just like yours. But I know she would have liked her.

Just like your mom would have liked Molly."

Champ nodded, still petting Molly. "It's hard when your mom is gone."

"It is. I'm glad we have good memories of our mothers."

He nodded again, then his eyes widened as he stood up. "I almost forgot. Would you like a drink? I have lemonade and water."

"I'm fine, but thank you."

"My mother taught me that, too. Always offer your guest something to drink."

"Your mom would be proud that you remembered."

Champ smiled for the first time since Kevin arrived, and he opened the curtains on both the windows before he sat on the floor again.

"I think Molly likes the sunshine."

Then Kevin remembered the main reason for the visit. "I was wondering if I could ask you a favor."

"Me?"

"Yes, a favor for Molly, really. Next Monday night, I'll be away. Just the one night. A work thing. Would you mind visiting Molly? She's fine, but she's really a social cat. She gets lonely."

"I would love to do that. Should I come on Tuesday after work, too?"

"That would be terrific, Champ—yes, both Monday and Tuesday if you don't mind. Her food and the litter box should be fine."

"I'll check both days," he said, then looked down. "We'll have fun, won't we Molly?"

Kevin smiled, and placed a key on the side table. "Here's the key. Works in the front or back door—just like all of our keys."

Once again, he felt badly that he'd originally thought of asking Ruth. Champ was the one who had a relationship with Molly. Still, there was that slight bit of anxiety.

Next time, Kevin decided. *Next time I'll ask about the boxes.*

Chapter 51

His skin was damp under his flannel jacket. Clearly the weather. A 50 percent chance of precipitation—snow and ice—but Evan wouldn't let that deter him this time. He was taking advantage of the open back roads, traveling 80 MPH in his uncle's truck, trying to tune in his radio to anything but talk shows. Once he hit the next town he'd jump on the highway. He was making good time—and nearly at the half-way point. Another four hours to go assuming no backups or weather issues.

When he spoke to his mother, he could hear a lift in her voice. It sounded lighter, like it had years ago, when the family was still complete. She was currently filling in as a substitute for a teacher on maternity leave, but insisted on taking the day off to spend time with him. That made Evan feel even guiltier. She thought he was coming to see her and his sisters. In fact, he was coming to destroy most of the box contents so the secret would remain that way.

What would Ruth think if she knew? He was glad that question would never need an answer. He allowed his mind to drift into areas previously shuttered. An engagement. Marriage. Starting a family of their own. They'd never discussed any of those things. He wasn't even sure Ruth wanted children. Or was ready for marriage, or even engagement. Although recently, she seemed different. Or maybe he was the one who'd changed.

He checked the gas gauge and decided to stop before the highway entrance. Last station on the back roads. The locally-owned station didn't advertise the brand of gasoline. Maybe they rotated, depending on the cost each week. As his uncle pulled him into more and more aspects of the marina, he realized success had as much to do with hard work as it did with ingenuity. He'd already contributed some cost-saving measures to the business, and had an idea for an e-commerce start-up. Of course, products were available online, but not everything in one place. Easy to order. Inexpensive. Full range of products. All through one user-friendly site. He'd tried out the idea on his uncle (from the marine business angle) and on Kevin (from the website side), and they'd been encouraging. Both suggested key issues to work through before moving forward. With his mind fixated on the box, he'd put the business on the back burner. He'd be able to move straight ahead soon.

At least he'd worked something out over the last few days. Why this fascination with Ruth? Originally, he'd reasoned that he and Ruth would have much in common. There would be a shared understanding, an emotional connection that no one else could understand. But that wasn't all. He didn't fault his father. He'd risked his life to save the family. But what he'd done hadn't been enough. He wasn't able to save himself. He wasn't able to save the Sagmires And he wasn't able to save Ruth.

Evan knew how painful it had been to lose his father. To think about him dying in the fire. But Ruth's pain was multiplied. Her father, mother, sisters, and brother. Who would save her from such a volume of pain? In his mind, he saw himself in that role. Who better, than someone who at least had a partial understanding.

The closer he grew to Ruth, the closer he realized his view was deeply flawed. She didn't need anyone to save her.

He was driving again. Thinking about the box. Thinking about his mother's need to constantly organize. To pull out things left underbeds, to find hidden notes tucked away. What if he opened the closet, pulled everything out, and it wasn't there? What if she'd looked at the contents and was waiting to talk with him in person? Last night, she'd sent him what he viewed as an ominous text:

Let's grab a drink before dinner so the two of us can talk

The text could be perfectly reasonable. This was the longest he'd gone without seeing his mother, and he'd never missed Christmas with his family. His sisters tended to take over all conversations, so maybe she just wanted time with her son. Maybe.

It was always a risk to read too much into a text. He ran through the most recent conversations with his mother. Was there something different in her voice? Something left unsaid?

He eased over to the highway entrance, his skin feeling sticky again, sweat dripping down the back of his neck. Maybe it wasn't the weather after all.

Chapter 52

As Evan eased the vehicle beside the grass that fronted the farmhouse, the door burst open. How long had his mother been waiting? Arms open. Smiling.

Inside, the house smelled like vanilla. No matter the season, his mother always had essential vanilla oil diffusing on the side table inside the entrance. The same side table and essential oil in their last home. Continuity.

"You're the one who made the long drive," she started. "What do you want to do? Sit here for awhile? Head out for a drink? There's a new craft brewery in town if you can believe it—something new at last."

"Sure, sounds great."

"Put your bag in your bedroom. Oh—I'll grab my keys. You've driven long enough."

Evan walked down the long, narrow hall and into his old room— third door on the right. As soon as he turned, he saw it. The box was sitting right on the red plaid bedspread. His breath caught in his throat.

"Oh," his mother started. "I found that box in the back of the closet. Thought you might want to take it."

He put his bag down on the chair, moved the box beside it.

As though reading his mind, she continued. "Don't worry—I didn't look inside. I figured the band was there for a reason."

He exhaled, realizing he'd been holding his breath. "Oh, thanks. I'll take it."

One thing his mother never did was lie. She sometimes held back information, but never actually lied. She didn't look inside the box. He'd relied on the thick rubber band and it somehow worked. The magic band.

She was pulling on her heavy coat when he returned, reaching back to lift her hair from inside the collar.

"Oh no," she continued. "I didn't want to see any folded up magazine pictures you might have in there! If I were you, I'd shred the contents. Don't want Ruth thinking you're still the same overheated teen."

"Overheated teen?"

She just looked at him.

"OK, probably accurate. You don't want me to drive mom? I can be your designed driver."

"Just one for me. Might have a second when we meet your sisters for dinner."

"Let's not get crazy, now! Two beers? Who are you? What's been happening since I've been away?"

She gave him a sideways look, lips pursed. "I guess you'll have to find out over a beer."

The man in her life. That's what she wanted to talk about. He already knew more than she'd expect. His aunt occasionally dropped some information, and his sisters provided even more. Dale Hanover. A widower. No children. Insurance Agent with his own business. Churchgoer. The only potential issue—he was 15 years older. But by all reports, a nice, gentle guy. A description that fit his father.

He would be nothing but positive when his mother shared the news. And Evan would pretend he didn't know anything—that the couple spent every Thursday evening at the new brewery. And on the first Tuesday of the month they attend the library book club. No— he would keep his poker face on. Although she'd probably figure it out. His mother was incredibly intuitive. Even her comment about destroying the contents of the box. Although she didn't guess the secrets hidden inside, somehow she knew they should never be revealed. And once again, like every other time he could remember, she was right. He didn't want her to know, and he especially didn't want Ruth to know. He didn't want anything, even the truth, to get in the way of their relationship.

Chapter 53

Champ walked home faster than usual. Today was Monday and Molly would be waiting for him. At the park where he stopped every day, he quickly placed the cat food in the bowl. not pausing to greet Brownie and Tannie, the friendliest of the stray cats who relied on him. He tossed a few peanuts behind the bench for the squirrels, then continued on his way.

"Hello there, Champ! Are you late for an appointment?" asked the flower shop owner who was sweeping a few stray leaves and pedals off the sidewalk.

"Not late, Mrs. Bloomsberry." he replied. "Just want to be on time. I have to help a friend with their cat."

"Good on you!" she called out, even though Champ was already too far ahead to hear her response.

Sometimes, he circled the block before Coastal View. There were a great number of dog owners on the block, and there was always an owner or two out for a walk. No time today. He walked straight ahead until he came to the entrance, not even stopping for the mail which was of little consequence since Champ often opened the box to see a single advertisement and sometimes nothing at all.

At the front door of Kevin's home, he looked inside the large front window to see if Molly was in view. She wasn't. In case she was standing at the door ready to bolt, he opened it just enough to poke his head inside, keeping his foot positioned to block the bottom.

Molly was sitting in the window above the kitchen sink. Kevin mentioned that she liked the spot, so he'd removed his herbs and placed them atop the refrigerator, with netting in place to keep her from eating the leaves.

Champ softly clapped his hands once and sat on the floor.

"Hello, Molly! I came to visit you today. Brought you a new toy," he said, putting his hand in his coat pocket and pulling out a pink mouse with feathers at the end of its tail. "Do you like pink?"

Champ dragged the feathers on the floor, making figure eights until Molly made two quick jumps—from the window to the counter and then to the floor. She pounced next to him, pawing at the feathers, then hopping to the other side and repeating. Eventually, Champ let go of the toy and held his open hands, palms out. Molly took the welcome and hopped on his lap.

"You are the friendliest girl ever. Sweet, sweet Molly," he said, repeating in a sing-song voice as she purred and rubbed against his stomach.

Time seemed to stand still for Champ and Molly, and then he remembered his instructions.

"OK, Molly. Your dad needs me to check your bowl," he said, standing and walking to the alcove that led to the back door. "Still a little more than half. Your dad said only fill if it goes below half."

He opened the back door, bringing in the bucket that sat on the step so he could clean the litter box, raking carefully until he was sure it was completely clear.

"There you go, Molly. Nice and clean for you," he said, replacing the scooper and then putting the bucket back on the step before locking the door.

In a flash, she was beside him again. As he touched her soft fur, he had an urge. Something he'd wanted to do for awhile. He remembered his mother's reminders about not acting quickly on urges.

"They may seem like a good idea to you, but not always to others."

Sometimes the advice didn't make sense, like when he tried to play dogs with the girls at school, or when he stood at the edge of the woods, watching Ruth's house burn, her family inside. But sometimes he saw people change when he acted on urges. Sometime a frown. Sometimes a shake of the head. Sometimes a quick retreat. So he trusted his mother. She was smarter and nicer than anyone he had ever known. She was even smarter and nicer than Kevin, and he was Champ's best friend. He wanted to ask his friend about this new urge, but he'd wait for a little while. If Kevin thought the urge was strange, he might lose his best friend and might not see Molly again. One thing Champ did know for sure. When he had an urge, it never went away.

Chapter 54

A full moon. There was something inspiring about a full moon over a graveyard. And so the digging continued as it did over the last three nights. A little at a time. He was fit, but not as strong as he was before, or maybe he was just more careful. The first time took just one night. Now he took three nights, four if the ground was hardened.

Sometimes the area was soft and soggy after spring rains. His mind told him to wait until the spring when the digging would be easier. But his heart told him the time was now. If he waited any longer, she'd be spoiled.

He sometimes wondered if the women knew how much he cared for them. How much he wanted to help them. He'd tried to explain it, but he wasn't sure they understood. Their eyes reflected a similar look. Anger, maybe. But fear, definitely. If only they knew he was saving them. Maybe this one would know. After all, she was older than the rest. Smarter. He needed to work quickly. She was changing.

Still, there was a comfort. She saw her family each time she left or returned to her house. Did she long to be with them? Now she would be reunited with her family—maybe not in the same grave but nearby.The last member of the family would be buried here beside the pet cemetery. Her family still incomplete.

There was no way to move her body to the family grave. At least not now. He would send a letter. Anonymously. With instructions on where to find her so she could be placed with her family. Even as he stood here, deciding on the next step, he knew he wouldn't take that risk. After his death, he decided. He'd find a way to leave a letter to be opened after his death.

Satisfied, he picked up the shovel and continued digging.

Chapter 55

Ruth arrived first, finding a corner table like she usually did when meeting Evan, who was due back from his family visit either late this evening or tomorrow. Yet another snow was due to start slowly tonight. In 24-hours the roads would be coated. She hoped he'd be home before travel was affected.

She'd had a reoccurring dream for years. She was at a train station, ticket in her hand, searching for the right train. The dream was frustrating. She ran up and down each set of tracks, searching for her train. When she woke, she'd be drenched in sweat. Two nights ago, she had the dream again. Only this time she found it. And when she turned, Evan was beside her. She took a single step, climbing onboard just as it started to move forward. But when she looked back, Evan was still on the platform.

"Deep in thought?"

"Hi Marjorie—I didn't notice you come in."

"Judging from your face, we have a lot to talk about."

"You aren't wrong. Are you sure you can't read my thoughts?"

After the waitress took their drink orders, Ruth settled back. "How's Augie? Did you two run off and elope?"

"I'm not that impulsive am, I?" Marjorie laughed. "Never mind—don't answer that! Augie is good. Really good."

Ruth wished she could say the same about Evan.

"Besides," Marjorie continued, "Would it be so crazy if we did elope? I mean, we've known each other for a long time."

"Not consecutively!"

"OK, there's that. And also the fact that we've only been dating for a month. I suppose we'll wait for you and Evan to get married first."

Ruth felt the heat on her face rising. She had a growing feeling that Evan might be ready to end the relationship. Just when she was ready to move forward.

"Here we go," the waitress said, placing their drinks on the table. "Ready to put in an order?"

"I'd like to start with your French onion soup," Marjorie said.

The waitress looked at Ruth.

"Make that two."

The bar was starting to fill, and Ruth distracted herself by taking a look around, even though she knew Evan wouldn't be here. She caught a glimpse of someone she knew, slightly surprised to see him here. At least she thought it was him. He'd turned in the other direction.

"Hello friend? Forgot I was here?"

"Sorry, Marjorie. I'm just a bit out of synch today."

"I noticed. Missing Evan?"

Ruth took another sip, delaying the answer. Truth was, she missed Evan—the old Evan. Or at least the old relationship.

"It's gotten complicated."

Marjorie just raised her eyebrows and leaned forward.

"Something's different. Different between the two of us. And I'm not sure what's different and how to fix it. Or if I can fix it."

"OK, let's take a step back. When did you notice a change?"

Ruth took a deep sigh and folded her hands it was time.

"I'll have to take a big step back. Years of steps back. Ready for a long story?"

"I have nowhere to go, my friend."

"The fire. It all goes back to the day of the fire."

Marjorie nodded. "We were together that night, the party. I've thought about it a lot over the years, but never wanted to bring it up. Figured you'd talk about it when you were ready."

"Did you know that Evan's father died in the fire? Trying to save my family?"

"Of course."

"Well, I didn't know."

Marjorie sat back, her eyes wide. "You didn't know? How is that—"

"I think my aunt tried to spare me the details. I really didn't know much at all about the fire as it turns out. And the little bit I thought I knew turned out to be wrong."

"I'm listening."

"Like what started the fire."

"Wasn't it electrical? Something about the wiring?"

Ruth shook her head. "You knew that?"

"I think my parents told me."

"No one told me—until just recently."

"Well," Marjorie started slowly, not sure where her friend was taking the story. "How did you think the fire started?"

The waitress appeared with two steaming bowls. "Careful, ladies— the bowls are really hot."

Ruth's hands were shaking as she carefully slid the bowl to the side, her appetite suddenly gone.

"I thought I was the one who started the fire."

Marjorie shook her head slowly. "But, Ruth! That's impossible. You were with me at the sleepover."

Ruth looked down, folding her still shaking hands on her lap. She looked up, tears in her eyes.

"I thought I'd left something plugged in. I left in such a hurry."

"And now you know that's not what happened?"

"I do. I finally talked to Father Anthony about it, and he suggested I meet with the Fire Chief. Of course he had all the records. Faulty wiring. It didn't even start in my bedroom—it started downstairs. The smoke rose and that's probably what...well, at least I can now imagine that the smoke ended their lives. Maybe while they were all still asleep."

"And now you can stop blaming yourself. Is that what you've been doing? All these years?"

Ruth was crying now, she pulled out a tissue to wipe her eyes, then took a couple sips of water.

She nodded. "That's what I thought."

Marjorie reached across the table to hold her hand. "If only I'd told you, Ruth. I would have saved you so much heartache. I'm so sorry."

"If only I talked to you about it Marjorie. If only I'd talked to anyone about it. Asked questions. It's no one's fault. I'm just glad to know the truth now. What's done can't be undone." Then a thought brightened the moment. "Besides, when I visited the Fire Chief that day, that's when I ran into Augie. Maybe it was all meant to be."

"I'm just sorry you suffered so all that time. But you're right—maybe it really was all meant to be," she said, then frowned. "And Evan? What's his involvement in all this? Did you tell him that you thought you were responsible?"

"I did. But not until I knew the truth. Do you think he's hurt I kept my feelings from him?"

"But you didn't share those thoughts with anyone, Ruth. And I suspect you only talked to Father Anthony because you were ready to move forward—whatever that meant."

"True," Ruth said. "After I found out the truth, I told Evan the story. He seemed fine at the time, but the next time I saw him, he seemed distant. And that's continued. The plan was to visit his family together in the spring, but he made a last-minute trip alone. I don't know what to make of it all."

"The mind of a man! I've never been able to figure out what to make of *that*. What goes on up there," she said, pointing to her temple. "It's a mystery for sure. But I think it may be less of a mystery than you think?"

"How so?"

"Again, I'm no expert in male-thinking, but I wonder if Evan decided to shift into serious mode. He realized you were ready to get serious, and now he's moving in that direction as well. Maybe he went home to talk to his mother about it."

"OK, I guess that's possible. I hadn't thought of it that way. You may have something there."

"Maybe I do know more about men's minds than I thought!"

The waitress stepped up to the table. "OK, ladies—I guess your soups are cool enough by now!"

"We took your advice to heart," Marjorie said.

"Refills?"

"Another round, please," Ruth said. She was in celebratory mood. Might be time to move beyond her self-imposed drink limit.

Chapter 56

He managed to stay out of sight, positioning himself at the last stool at the bar, just beside the hallway that led back to the kitchen, restrooms, and emergency exit. She'd used the rest room once, and he had done the same—moving ahead of her to be sure he was inside the men's room before she reached the bar. He'd listened from inside until she exited, then waited a minute before returning to the bar. Twice, she glanced in his direction, and he'd turned toward the wall. He was hyper vigilant, expecting her to turn at any moment. Instead, she focused on the conversation with her friend and the drink in front of her. Drinks. The first time he'd watched her, a few months ago, she'd only had one. Life was already on a path to destroy her innocence.

His mother had taught him to be prepared so he didn't react before thinking. Which is why he had the plan. The plan that worked every time.

She was standing now, walking outside with her friend. He'd already settled the bill when she'd done the same, and he fell back into the hall as she passed. Through the glass doors, he saw her beneath the streetlight, hugging her friend as they moved in separate directions. He followed at a good pace behind but kept her in view. The darkness, and the dimness of the streetlamps gave him easy cover.

She stumbled a bit on a raised sidewalk--the big root from the oak tree pushing it up. She wouldn't have noticed in the dark. Or maybe if she'd limited herself to one drink. Soon, all the innocence would be gone. And there would be no way to save her. He forced himself to stop his mind from drifting. *Focus on the plan.*

This was the intersection where they'd part ways. He sprinted down the sidewalk. No outside cameras on this street, he'd confirmed just last week. He took a left at the alley, running until he reached the end. Another left and he was on the route she always followed home. He'd followed her twice to be certain. His car awaited.

The trunk was closed, but not latched. He reached inside and pulled out the rag and bottle from the side, feeling in the darkness. He quietly tapped the trunk closed and waited. Just a few seconds now, he thought, judging from her pace, slower when she drank. He heard the strains of her voice—a song. She wasn't close enough for him to make out the tune, but soon she would be. At the precise spot he'd selected. The spot with the burned-out streetlight. The spot without houses in view.

He could hear his heart pounding in his ears like it always did. He liked to imagine it was louder each time. The combined beat from the hearts of all the young women he had saved. He shifted for a better view, his eyes adjusted to the dark.

As she passed the passenger's side of his car he stood, his hand with the soaked rag behind his back as he stepped forward.

"Oh, Granston! What are you—"

In what was a series of movements, but so seamlessly executed Granston felt they were just one single movement, he placed the rag over her mouth. She wriggled, and then she relaxed. She stilled so quickly, more quickly than the others, and Granston grabbed her waist so she didn't fall. With his free hand, he opened the back passenger door, and lifted her inside the dark vehicle. He'd turned the overhead lights off earlier. He heard an engine, followed by lights. A car was turning down the street, coming in their direction. The heartbeat in his head deafening his ability to reason. He crouched down in the back, pulling the door behind him. He waited until he couldn't hear the noise from the engine, then reached down in the dark for the twine.

He tied her legs together then reached across to tie her hands and stuff a dry rag in her mouth. He placed her purse on the front seat and pulled out her phone, an inconvenient piece of evidence that might identify her last location. He left location one and drove down the street in the direction she was walking. He continued to an area designed state and county parkland, with no houses, no cameras. He reached an even more remote area—location 2—and threw her purse into the brush. Originally, he'd thought to plant the purse in Champ's residence, but decided not to bring even more attention to the community.

He turned the car to backtrack his drive. For a split second, he thought he sensed movement in the backseat. He turned, but Ruth was completely still. Maybe she'd slid on the seat. He hoped she wouldn't worry. It was hard for them to understand that he was doing this for them. If only someone had the courage to do this for his sister. She was missing for two years before the sheriff arrived, hat tucked under his arm. That somber look. Her body was found during an investigation into a series of slain prostitutes. Granston's mother was never the same. Even in her last days she cried out her daughter's name.

"You'll be safe with the other girls, Ruth," he said softly. "And with your family."

Coastal View was quiet, as expected. The porch light was on at Ruth's house. Evan's house was completely dark, and all the lights were all on at Kevin's. He was aware that Kevin was working late tonight—key to his plan. Through the front window, he saw Champ on the sofa looking down, so focused on the cat he didn't even look up.

Granston continued to the back of Loretta and Lou's, location 3, and glanced at his watch: 9:10. The only wildcard—he wasn't sure what time Champ would leave Kevin's house. But Granston would keep close watch until he moved to location 4. The grave was ready. He'd also checked out the view from Kevin's house while he was at work one day last week. No view of Loretta and Lou's back property.

He jumped out of the driver's side, unlocked the back door, and opened it a crack before returning to his car. He pulled Ruth out slowly. He carried her quickly into the house and laid her on the thick plastic he'd placed on the floor earlier that day. He'd return later to clean up. He'd have plenty of time since Loretta and Lou would be away for some time. As usual, he'd taken every precaution—gloves, phone relocation, plastic on his backseat and floor, situational awareness. No potential witnesses. Although if any emerged, he had his gun and a silencer.

Now he waited. The waiting was hard, but it would lead to the next part. The next part was what distinguished him from serial killers. Just like he did with the others, he would tell Ruth he was saving her. Most of the girls cried or tried to scream. Not Ruth. She was older than the rest. She wanted to see her family. Yes, Ruth would understand. He was her savior. He glanced at her again. Patience.

Chapter 57

Ruth was awake and had been since some point in the car ride. She'd read enough mysteries to quickly comprehend what was happening when she smelt what must have been chloroform. And so, she instantly relaxed. When she started to wake, she was woozy, but could feel the rope on her wrists and ankles. A gag in her mouth. So from the backseat she took the only approach she could. She would remain immobile until the right moment.

Inside now, she'd managed to slightly loosen the rope around her wrist. She knew he'd be watching, but when she heard him walk back outside, she worked on the rope. She arranged herself just slightly so she could hide her wrists, but not change her position so much that he would know. She heard the car door shut and she continued to work the rope. But once the back door opened she became immobile again.

He couldn't see her mind working:

1. Loosen the ropes enough to slip out her wrists

2. Untie the rope around her ankles

Of course, step 2 relied on Granston leaving at some point. She focused her mind—there was no reason to think that he wouldn't step away—even a moment could give her enough time.

3. Run out the back or front door…or lock the bedroom door and call for help from the side window…find a weapon.

Step 3 would depend on the situation. If Granston stepped out the back door she might have a chance to run out the front and over to Kevin's. If Granston was still in the house, she would lock the door and call for help. Or find a weapon. But even as she thought through the options, she knew finding a weapon to compete with the gun Granston was certainly carrying wouldn't be feasible. *What's he going to do with me?*

She forced herself to clear those thoughts from her mind. She always believed her family was watching over her—even when she thought she was responsible for their deaths. She felt her prayers carried more weight somehow, like her family was prompting God to take care of her. And so she prayed. She prayed for a clear mind. Strong body. Opportunity. Bravery.

Oh God, make me brave. Make me brave like my family. Like Evan's father. Just a small part of their bravery for this one night. I don't want to die.

And then she heard a sound. Granston's footsteps. A door closing. The bathroom.

Ruth's wrists were nearly out already. She wriggled out one hand and then the other. She immediately started on her ankles, but they were harder to loosen. She pulled at the rope and it started to give way, slightly. But not enough to free her ankles. The door was opening again. So Ruth returned to the same position, loosened the rag in her mouth so she could easily thrust it out with her tongue, and positioned the rope over her wrists. And she waited.

Granston stepped over to the doorway. Satisfied, he returned to his spot on the sofa, for the hardest part—waiting. Once more, he reminded himself that the plan worked. It had worked nine times before. And it would work the tenth time.

Ruth and Granston heard it at the same time. A car engine. He stepped over to the window, mumbling.

"What the hell, are you kidding me? How did…"

She heard him move quickly to the back door, and she was already working the knot on her ankles. Once more, she tried in vain to slide one of her feet out through the slightly loose rope. She was nearly out when she heard Granston return. Discouraged, she settled into her position again.

"Damn kids," Granston muttered. It had been some time, but an occasional teenager on a date would drive through the graveyard, somehow figuring out the gate code. Now he'd have to wait for them to leave before he changed locations. He checked his watched again: 9:26. She would wake up soon. Still enough time.

On the floor, Ruth continued her prayer. *One more distraction. And a chance to be brave.*

She couldn't hear the car anymore. Maybe they'd left. She reminded herself. *Be patient. Stay alert. Be ready.*

Granston could hear an imaginary clock in his head. Tick, tick, tick. It was almost time. He fiddled with everything he could. Checking his watch. Unlatching and latching his belt. Patting his gun.

The car. Once again, and this time driving right by the house, circling in the opposite direction.

Granston made his way to the back door again. He could get in his car and pull them over, but he didn't want to. Instead, he moved to the side of the house and waited to see if this was their last pass. He hated leaving Ruth, but she wasn't going anywhere.

Inside, Ruth was still working on the rope. Moving her finger inside to tug. One ankle was out, and then the other. She stood, feeling slightly woozy.

The sound of the car was gone, and as she stepped toward the front door, she heard the back door open.

Ruth twisted the knob, but it wouldn't open. *The deadbolt lock.* With no other alternatives, she started to turn, but he was already there. He grabbed her left arm to control her, and as he did, she reached up with her left hand and grabbed the only weapon in reach.

She snapped the bulky silver cross from its chain and with all the strength she could summon, stabbed the pointed end into his eye. Granston released her arm and bent over, both hands instinctively guarding his eye.

Ruth ran past him, and out the unlocked back door. Screaming as she ran. "Help! I need help!"

The lights were on at Kevin's and she raced toward the front, hoping the car might still be in the area in case Granston followed her.

Between labored breaths, she was still calling out as she rounded the front, taking the first step toward the front porch. She felt his arm, pulling her backward and she grabbed the rail, trying to hold on until Kevin came out to help her.

Chapter 58

Champ heard the first cry for help. His mother's voice echoed in his head. *When someone needs help, call the police.* The first time she told him that was the night of the fire. The night when Champ had stood at the edge of the woods helplessly.

He hit the emergency dial for 911.

"What's your emergency? Police, fire, ambulance?"

"All three," Champ said. "Hurry!"

He stayed on the line as instructed but walked to the front window. Granston was trying to hurt Ruth.

He was afraid, but he knew Ruth needed him. He unlocked the front door and as he opened it, shouted into the phone, "It's Deputy Granston. He's trying to hurt Ruth!"

He kept the phone connected and stepped out on the porch. "They know—I told them. They know it's you," Champ shouted. "It's Granston," he said again into the phone.

Granston pulled his gun from the holster. "I didn't want it to come to this," he said, his left hand awkwardly holding her arm as he pushed her up the steps. She stepped back with her right foot and hooked it on the edge of the step, shifting her weight suddenly. As they both fell off the steps, Ruth's face hit the edge of the last step before she fell into the dirt, next to Granston.

She could taste blood from the cut on her lip. "Go inside, Champ! Lock the door!" But Champ didn't move.

Granston was standing now. Pointing his gun at Ruth. "We're going inside, both of you. I don't want to shoot you but I will."

He grabbed Ruth's arm and yanked her on her feet. And as he roughly pushed her onto the steps, she heard a sound. A siren. Granston heard it too, and stood still for a moment, suddenly frozen. He'd have to abandon the plan.

As he turned, Ruth ran up the steps and steered Champ back into the house. With the key still in his hand, he locked the door. She ran to the back to be sure the other door was locked and then heard two sounds—the siren growing closer and a car starting. Granston was getting away.

Chapter 59

Granston had a plan. But his plan didn't factor in quick thinking Ruth, or bold Champ, whose identification during the 911 call led to apprehension. Granston's careful plan also didn't consider the fire engine which blocked the single exit point from Coastal View.

Ruth's testimony, her recollection from the back seat of his reference to "other girls" lead investigators on a search, which ended in the closed pet cemetery. They didn't mention the empty grave to the press, seemingly to spare Ruth at least for the moment since that information would likely emerge at trial.

Today's party was overdue, but pushed back several times to ensure Lou could attend, following a couple of setbacks. Now three months after the incident, the neighbors were ready to celebrate and Rafferty Enterprises even paid for the party.

Kevin and his now semi-serious girlfriend Chelsea, who owned a party planning business had arrived early to decorate. The beginning of the party would be for residents only. A time to relax and enjoy each other in a spacer larger than their usual tiny house gatherings. After the first hour, guests would arrive, including the mayor. Unbeknownst to him, Champ would be honored as Heritage Man of the Year.

Ruth had chosen the theme—family—because she realized now her neighbors were more than friends. They were family. Even decided to take that theme a step further, and with each resident's permission and help, enlarged photos of each one posing with their families.

The largest wall in the banquet room was divided into six sections. Champ's section was the first and featured one photo with both his parents, another with just his mother, and a third with one of his cats. It was that picture that reminded Champ to ask Kevin if he could clip off a section of hair from Molly for his collection. When he'd explained the boxes, Kevin just nodded, a feeling of relief washing over him.

Loretta and Lou's section, although separate, included a large picture that spanned both sections, taken a month ago when they gathered for dinner. The photo included their three children and six grandsons, including Michael, smiling broadly and standing between his grandparents. There was a second picture of their granddaughter Sonia, taken in the incubator before she passed.

Ruth's section followed, with two pictures that came from her aunt. One with her whole family, and a second with just her little brother. Ruth had declined interviews for both print and broadcast outlets, trying to focus all the attention to Champ, who as it turns out, was more of a champion than he (or his father) ever imagined. But Ruth knew who the other hero was. Her brother Sam, who had selected his last Christmas gift to her from the second-hand shop. A large, heavy silver crucifix with a pointed tip on the bottom.

Kevin's area featured several photos of his family of four, taken over three decades. He'd also included two separate twin pictures—one when they were babies, and another more recent picture.

"I just love this one of you and Kia," Chelsea remarked as she fixed it on the wall. "Maybe I'll get to meet her soon?"

Kevin smiled, "I'd like that."

The last section was Evan's. He'd chosen a picture of the family before his father's death, another with his mother and siblings, and one with his aunt and uncle. But the largest picture was him and Ruth, standing in front of the marina, her head resting on his shoulder as she looked down at her left hand, the diamond catching light from the sun.

Acknowledgments

To my family for their inspiration and support: my husband Tony, daughters Sarah and Christa, son-in-law Alex. And to my precious granddaughter Frankie Jean whose mere presence shows me the immense beauty and joy of life.

To my candid and thoughtful beta readers Cindy Jaimieson, Sarah Stramella, Nancy Shugars (my greatest cheerleader!), and Terry Kostkowski; proofreader Chris Goss; and copy editor Charlie Stein. Any remaining errors are my own.

To a couple of key experts: Anji Curry, who reviewed my depictions of Philadelphia; and Jimmy Siebert, a retired firefighter who reviewed details about the fire (thanks also to Diana Boyd for the contact). Any remaining errors are my own.

To the men who told me similar "car stories" from which Kevin's fictional depiction was based.

To my fellow author friends who provide encouragement, information, and comradery along the solitary writing path: Linda

Murphy-Marshall, Gerry Winter, Elizabeth Gauffreau, Carol LaHines, James White, Keith Madsen, Joyce Yarrow, Toni Morgan, Rita Baker, John Casey, and Jim Metzner. To all at Quill Hawk Publishing, especially its energetic and wise publisher Amy M. Le; and to illustrator Virginia McKevitt.

For the missing and their families. The advocacy group Native Hope reports thousands of missing American Indian and Alaska Native women and girls.

And finally, to my parents Marion and Milton Koros whose love still makes all things possible, and to my God who continues to open my heart a little more each day.

About the Author

Donna Koros Stramella is a writer from Maryland whose fiction and nonfiction pieces have been published in various literary magazines and anthologies. She is a previous award-winning journalist, scriptwriter, newspaper columnist, and government communication strategist. A graduate of the University Tampa MFA in Creative Writing, she is the author of *Coffee Killed My Mother*.

Donna Koros Stramella

www.ingramcontent.com/pod-product-compliance
Lightning Source LLC
Chambersburg PA
CBHW061238310726
48971CB00007B/2115